Literary Story as an Art Form:
A Text for Writers

William H. Coles

AuthorHouse™
1663 Liberty Drive, Suite 200
Bloomington, IN 47403
www.authorhouse.com
Phone: 1-800-839-8640

First published by AuthorHouse 6/25/2008

ISBN: 978-1-4343-9158-2 (sc)

Library of Congress Control Number: 2008905388

Printed in the United States of America
Bloomington, Indiana

This book is printed on acid-free paper.

CONTENTS

Part I
Essence

Chapter 1: *The Literary Fictional Story*

Chapter 2: *Preparing to write the great literary story*

Chapter 3: *How Literary Stories Go Wrong*

Chapter 4: *Character in Literary Fiction*

Chapter 5: *Credibility in Literary Fiction*

Chapter 6: *1ˢᵗ person POV in Literary Story*

Chapter 7: *Narration of Literary Stories*

Chapter 8: *Information and Literary Story Structure*

Chapter 9: *Drama in Literary Fiction*

Chapter 10: *Desire and Motivation in Literary Fiction*

Chapter 11: *Momentum in Literary Fiction*

Chapter 12: *Parting Thoughts Part I*

Part II
Creating a Literary Story

A. Process of Creating a Story

B. Sample Story "The Indelible Myth"

Literary Story as Art:
A Text for Writers

Part I
Essence

Chapter 1

The Literary Fictional Story

Definitions
Elements
Imagination

Structure and theme

Characterization

Plot

Success

Philosophy
Goals

Drama

Entertain

Fame and fortune

The essence

The Literary Fictional Story

Definitions

Story—an account of an event or a series of events.
Fictional—creating imaginary people or events.
Literary— important writing with permanent and memorable artistic value.

Elements

Imagination

Literary story is imagined; it is not a memoir that tells a happening that the narrator knows occurred or has experienced. Although a real happening can stimulate the imagination for the basis of a literary story, to present a memoir story as a fictional story loses the potential of imagination-based creative elements. Imagination allows growth of characterization, motivation, setting, and provides a special memorable experience for the reader.

Structure and theme

The author of literary fiction explores the imagination for just the right story elements to describe an event in a series of scenes. The author then structures the story and establishes a thematic goal that will influence character and plot development. Structure augments desires, motivations, and credibility by focusing and integrating the writing; structure intensifies reader engagement and perceptions of meaning.

Characterization

Characters of the literary story must be interesting, complex and developed, and contribute to the story with author-controlled prioritization. The author creates each character's emotional story line to fit in with motivations and actions of all characters, and to contribute to plot momentum.

The characters in a literary story are unique, yet they are not bizarre. They have heroic characteristics, but they are not super-heroes with powers beyond the limits of human expectation.

In good stories, the reader has thorough knowledge of who the characters are and why they do what they do. The reader follows a progressive unity of characterization that focuses on the story, and the development of characters is always consistent with story conflict-resolution. In essence, story resolution must be in accord with everything the characters have done in the story. That is the essence of story telling.

Plot

A literary story has a character driven plot with carefully developed and sequenced motivations that is presented through scenes structured with conflict, action, and resolution, and results in sufficient reader emotional involvement to cause (1) enlightenment or (2) reversal of thinking.

Success

Successful storytelling depends on the author's personal traits, beliefs, and opinions. But the author is not part of the story. A literary story demands an author's willingness to imagine the most effective characterization and plot motives to assure story momentum and to achieve reader delight.

Philosophy

To reach maximum success with a literary story, authors of fiction must discover who they are and why they write. In many ways, the telling of fictional stories is a performance that can be damaged or destroyed by ill-conceived attitudes about writing.

Goals

The ultimate success of a story is to evoke emotion in the reader without sentimentality. Authors must engage the reader early in the story so the reader experiences the story, and does not just follow the events. This is difficult to achieve as it may happen to some readers and not others, and it occurs in various degrees with different readers reading the same words.

Multiple factors heighten reader experience. There must be character development that allows the reader to strongly connect early. The reader must respect and sympathize with the character, if not like. Characters must be more than ordinary. Trivial characters, and writing, do not support a memorable reader experience. Characters must have an identifiable strong desire that will justify motivations. The story must have a theme and meaning so that the reader not only experiences the story, but, through the emotion, is enlightened about some aspect of the human condition—either new or reinforced.

Drama

Great stories are dramatically constructed art forms—a sculpture in words—that produce enlightened change in characters and readers. Stories are not beautiful descriptions of abstractions lived—such as love, hate, revenge, or jealousy. And stories are not created to purge the author of an emotional or intellectual crisis. Stories are also not character sketches or detailed descriptions of events that moved the author to experience emotion. Stories are characters with strong desires, acting to resolve conflict in meaningful ways. Through drama, the reader is right in the conflict with the characters—and discovering meaning too.

In contrast, the dramatic literary story is not memoir (non-fictional writing), which is a popular and legitimate form of writing. But writing a memoir requires skills that often conflict with imaginative fiction. Adherence to the truth of what happened or the belief that a story based on a true story is equal to, or superior to, the created fictional story, are destructive attitudes for the goals of a fiction writer. Most great stories are not just told from life; great stories are ideas (that may be stimulated by life) successfully expressed by creating a dramatic (and significant) series of fictional events.

Entertain

Fictional stories entertain and enlighten through drama—drama is conflict, action, and resolution. Readers become involved in the story; readers do not simply observe the story. To repeat, the writer's challenge is to engage the reader from story beginning to end, not to describe events. The writing must also be succinct. Successful writers actually provide only enough information on the page to stimulate the reader's mind. It is one of the wonders of reading great fictional stories that, for each reader, the interpretation of the story is unique to that reader and based on the reader's intelligence, experience, and creativity.

To persuade a reader to a preset opinion does not support the creation of a great story. Authors enlighten about human nature; essayists, editorialists, and columnists persuade readers to adopt opinions. Fiction authors who insert unrelated opinions in their stories face the danger of having their work labeled as propaganda (deceptive or distorted information often about policy, ideas, doctrines, or causes). This topic is sensitive. Modern editors and publishers may see fiction immersed in the immediate political opinions of the day as writing that is more profitable that the beautifully constructed literary story. Lasting artistic excellence can be rejected for mass appeal of the moment.

Fame and fortune

Literary fiction is not an easy road to either fame or fortune. Two reasons play an important role: authors who write literary stories have fewer readers than authors of commercial fiction and nonfiction, and editorial and publishing decisions often favor genre and memoir writing in place of, or instead of, literary fiction. Still, there is a need for the literary story as an art form. The creative achievement alone seems to reward those serious authors who are dedicated, obsessed, and who see literary fiction as a valuable art form. These authors serve those readers who find enjoyment in the literary story.

Still, authors want recognition for their work and the literary fiction writer may consider writing to the desires of a specific editor or publisher. Often this means writing with a genre plot-emphasis—a significant achievement, but not literary fiction. Desire for fame as an author that results in marketing and self-promotion imposes restrictions on the creation of a great story. Writing a literary story is a selfless process. Unsuccessful writers should not sell their souls to the promotion of inferior stories, especially to the uninformed, as worthy examples of art.

The essence

Write a literary story as a unit, not as loosely associated ideas discovered moment by moment. Don't allow prose to become overwrought. Stories fail because of ineffective characterization or incredible conflicts and actions. Stories rarely fail because the prose is not fancy enough. Yet most authors revise through prose adjustment in style and craft when valuable revision most often comes from structural adjustment, clarity of intent, and idea change.

Chapter 2

Preparing to write the great literary story

A. Introduction

B. Key Elements of Good Stories

    1. *Drama in storytelling.*

    2. *Desire.*

    3. *Balance of Narrative with In Scene Action.*

    4. *Back story.*

        Example 1: no back story.

        Example 2: back story.

    5. *Humor.*

    6. *Meaning.*

    7. *Morality.*

    8. *Significance.*

    9. *Emotions.*

Preparing to write the great literary story

A. Introduction

An author of literary fiction must absorb:

(1) Craft (skill in doing things). The craft of writing must emphasize clarity and readability in the product. Learning craft is a continuous process that makes the quality of the writing progress throughout a writer's career. Although mastery of craft is essential to great stories, too many writers work hard on craft and ignore other important elements of story telling in their development.

(2) Story telling. Story telling is more subjective than the more technical aspects of craft and is often harder to learn.

(3) Drama. Drama through the written word is the foundation for successful literary fiction as an art form. To create drama, characterization and character-driven plot must be vivid and imaginative. The conflict and action and meaningful resolution, the elements of drama, are instilled in the writing.

(4) Characterization. Every major character should be created as if that character will be unique, memorable, and a lasting presence in the collective conscience of educated readers.

(5) Cause and effect in plot. Plot is everything that happens in a story (and not what is described). Since stories are a series of events told in scenes, these events must be related, always by cause and effect—a swing-the-bat-to-hit-the-ball kind of thinking. Although often combined with elements of character and theme development, and the momentum inherent in the story, plot cause and effect in any scene should be understood by the reader.

B. Key Elements of Good Stories

1. *Drama in storytelling.*

Drama is conflict, action, and resolution. For intense drama, the desires of the characters must be significant and based logically on the foundation of character development. In literary fiction, dramatic conflict is more effective among believable and respected characters, rather than super-heroes facing abstract, inanimate threats like asteroids on a collision path with earth.

The concept of dramatic writing that is engaging is not easily conceived or easily ingrained in the writing process. Although complex, the most important skills for dramatic development are related to character development and creating scenes that contribute to the story in interesting ways. Most failure in creating drama occurs when authors strive for emotions in the characters—and in the readers—with description, rather than creating the emotions through actions and conflicting desires.

Description is an easy trap for a writer. Too much description is often a sinkhole for a reader. Description is dependent on language manipulation, and not on logical character action. Instead of description, authors must learn to frequently involve the reader in the story action by showing the action through a character or narrator, rather than having a character or narrator describing action or environment. Literary examples can point the way, but only practice and discovery can affect learning.

Poets can be great storytellers, but storytellers are not primarily poets, and the belief that lyrical prose alone creates a great story is antithetical to reality. Writing effective literary stories does not depend on how lyric the descriptive prose, or how erudite, or how difficult ideas are to access. Great fiction is primarily in scene action with clear, logical thinking. Of course lyrical prose can be clear and logical and support a story, but it cannot compete with a reader's enjoyment of the story as a result of stagnation in the dramatic action.

The key for writers is to understand the deference between describing a feeling—love, anger, jealousy, etc.—and creating these feelings through action and conflict. This is the major differentiation between a literary story and character sketches or memoirs. For a fiction writer who engages a reader to a point where emotions are stirred, dramatic action is the most important tool.

2. *Desire.*

Think of the desire that motivates in conflict, action, and resolution rather than image and setting. How does a character respond to major and minor events? There is a common belief that authors should strive in their writing for a moment where the character creates the story on the page. Teachers imply some mystical, intracranial invasion of the author by the character, almost supernatural, that frees the writer to let the character do the work. However, character takeover is a harmful goal. In terms of the literary story, where success in creating an art form requires control of story structure and meaning, when the character creates story, the thrust of the story and the meaning often begin to float untethered. For reader satisfaction, everything that happens to a character in a story needs to have a purpose and be within the full control of the author.

The core desire of a character must be more intense and focused than in real life. In life, it is not possible to sustain intense desire that interacts and emerges differently throughout life. In determining the core desire of a character, particularly a major character, the desire should focused, and not be abstract. "He wanted love" is an abstract desire, understandable for a living human but not honed enough for a character driving the plot in a literary story. Instead, something more specific and energized is needed. "Unattractive since childhood, ridiculed by the girls in his school for gross features, and always believing that his mother preferred his two brothers to him, he longed for the admiration of a woman, any woman, who could know and accept him for who he was." Or: "He needed intimacy, intimacy no one could ever verbalize, intimacy that was only achievable through the physical and spiritual contact with a woman, intimacy that seemed infinitesimal and eternal." Even these examples don't seem right, and show the difficulty of finding a reasonable and intense core desire for a character. In practice, part of the core desire may only be discovered after the character develops to a certain level.

Authors need in-depth thinking, with choices made about characters' desires and subsequent motivations, before sitting down to write. Motivations must be significant, logical, and appropriate for the conflict, action, and resolution of the story. Motivations must also be right for the scene, for the logical and synergistic actions with motivations in all other scenes, and consistent with the development and progressive understanding of the motivation at any time in the story. This demands consideration of the structure and the interactions of all the characters in a story.

Character motivation in a story is never static. It is always changing, like hundreds of vipers in a pit; each snake, at any instant, has a unique relationship to every other, and that relationship will change in the next instant, wiggling, advancing, and regressing, until the moment ends.

3. *Balance of Narrative Description with In Scene Action.*

Effective narrative description is necessary for great fiction, but excessive narrative description is tempered (not eliminated) in great writing. Narrative passages allow for a condensation of time that will increase the reader's feeling of movement through story time. The pace of the story has more possibilities than in the more restrictive in-scene action passage. Narrative description also allows extended and continuous action to be summarized, which captures the interest of readers. When lyrical passages (including summary, stream of consciousness, and internal reflection) are needed in the presentation for enjoyment in the reading, narrative description is often the best way to create the desired effect.

However, narrative description can be seductive to an author. For most authors, narrative description is easier to write—more intuitive—and it tends to be overdone. As a general rule, narrative description should have a story purpose; it should develop character or move plot, and must not be a vehicle for inflated prose.

In great stories, theme and meaning are often more effectively transmitted by emotional discovery rather than intellectual explanation. Essentially, this means showing and not telling—in-scene and not with narrative description and summary, using concrete and not abstract thinking and writing, creative process and not descriptive process; and structure of characters' responses that relate to story rather than random reflections on abstruse thoughts.

4. *Back story.*

In most great stories, back story is avoided by structuring the story form so the front story is advancing without interruption. Back story should only be employed in a story when it is necessary to advance the front story. In addition, when writing back story, the timeline of the story is shifted to a time before the story's beginning. This often deadens the effectiveness of the passage. Compare these two examples—awkward and over written to make a point. There seems to be a definite shift in momentum when back story is used to provide essentially the same information in the passage which does not rely on back story.

Example 1: no back story.

The curtain parted just far enough for Maria to step forward into the spotlight and then closed. She bowed to the audience's applause and cupped one hand in the other in a gesture of formality to lead to the opening note of the aria. She nodded to the piano player who, after a pause, started playing. The first notes sharpened her expectation of the note she needed. He was playing introductory chords now. Maria listened for the cue to pinpoint her starting notes, that always difficult major seventh so peculiar and unique to this composer. My God. The pianist has skipped the refrain with her critical cue note. She must have the cue. He was new, but no mistakes could be tolerated. He was headed for her beginning. How could he ignore her cue? Maybe he would still return and do it right. She glared, now trying to make eye contact. He plodded on. The audience turned into a thousand hostile critics instead of an adoring group of friends she liked to imagine. He was seven bars from her entrance. Here it comes. God! She took a deep breath, searching her memory for some clue to the starting pitch.

Example 2: back story.

The curtain parted just far enough for Maria to step forward into the spotlight and then closed. She bowed to the audience's applause and cupped one hand in the other in a gesture of formality to lead to opening note of the aria. She nodded to the piano player. He started the intro. She had met with him briefly yesterday. He was a dull and sullen young man, though attractive with dark brown eyes and a scraggly black bard. She had carefully explained how she needed the refrain in the intro before the aria. She could only start when she heard the fifth to orient her to the nonchordal tone that the composer insisted on using. They had practiced, in the short time available, only the passages themselves. She thought he had understood. Now he'd forgotten the refrain. He finished the intro and went directly to the verse. She felt the panic rise in her. There was no way she could hit the note. And there was no way she could not go forward. She felt the audience's expectant stares. She heard their breathing. When she sang the note, the pianist's head jerked toward her. He knew what he had done.

Comment. In the back story, there is a slowing down of front story action, without back story contributing to front story in any special way. (Part of the slowing down is augmented by the lackluster style of the writing example to make a point). For most writing, back story is more detrimental than additive. Usually, back story information should be incorporated seamlessly into the story through restructuring.

5. *Humor.*

The effect of humor in its many forms is different for every human. Why today, for example, can a skillful comic slip on a banana peel and provoke many smiles and laughs from a diverse audience, even when it's a worn cliché of a repetitive action? Why do people laugh at the painful, degrading, or humiliating situations of others? Humor is difficult to define, but humans, and characters, show essential values and desires in what they find funny. At times, humor is a way of releasing tension, and often humor acts as a foil to more serious thoughts and feelings that may be unstated. Whatever the origins of humor, a sense of humor is important in character development.

Irony (a form of humor where what happens is not what might be expected) is a more subtle form of humor and essential for good fiction. In-depth exploration of human needs and expectations as well as a clear understanding of social interactions must be developed.

6. *Meaning.*

Meaning and theme in literary fiction are essential to change or reverse an existing way of thinking about something (enlightenment). Meaning takes on more significance as a story goal when the change or reversal in thinking is associated with a feeling that the world will never be exactly the same as it was before the enlightenment.

Characters change during storytelling in meaningful ways. It is part of successful dramatic structure that includes expert character development. But it is the reader's awareness of meaning, at times not articulated or even formed as a complete concept that represents the success of the author of literary stories.

7. *Morality.*

All writing is strengthened by a concept of what is moral (issues of right and wrong). In essence, character actions and thinking exist in a moral cobweb. This morality need not be spiritually or legally correct, but it must be consistent for the story, and the moral cobweb established must control logical actions in the story. However, morality is formative, not controlling. Authors who feel strongly about a moral view, usually their view, may impose on the reader an almost threatening challenge to accept their attitudes. This is not useful in storytelling, where concepts of morality are used for desires and motivations of characters rather than saving the reader from damnation.

8. *Significance.*

Literary stories have the possibility, and maybe even the responsibility, to be significant. A literary story helps the reader deal with the great mysteries of life: Who are we? Why are we here? What are we supposed to do? What comes after?

These questions are always with all humans, to various degrees of consideration, during conscious life. Through the well-written literary story, a reader may discover something that shows him or her about the human condition, and help discover what purpose humans have in living and dying. This is not about philosophy, or abstract social restrictions; it is about learning through the acting and thinking of believable characters how we can deal with the unknowns, and how we can justify our existence to superiors we cannot prove exist. A great literary story can help us to just be human.

9. *Emotions.*

Emotions are hard to define. In fact, emotions' value to writers is their omnipresence in humans and characters, and the variable reactions they evoke. However, emotions can be a semantic nightmare, forcing each author to identify his or her own emotional palette for use in creating stories.

Emotions may be paired as opposites such as sadness/joy, love/hate, and anger/fear, etc. This is to think about emotions as spectra isolated from overall human responses and identified and paired down for creating stories. For most situations, emotions seem to be more like emulsions than separate vials, and when a character seems to act with complex, yet identifiable, feelings, the characterization may be more effective.

You might also define emotions as to the reaction produced: laughing, crying, flight, or fight. This is useful for scene action, but tends to be superficial for characterization without other considerations that provide more depth into character feelings.

You may just think of what might be core emotions (lust, fear, delight, distress) and then fit other sensations such as depression, contentment, satisfaction, irritation, etc. into categories. This is valuable thinking to be sure that, as you structure a story, emotions will be reasonable for the character you've established, and that the actions generated by certain emotions are logical. Structure helps, while writing random ideas as they flow into the mind lends to unbelievable storytelling.

The emotions valuable to the writer are usually lasting, rather than transient. For example, anger is inferior to deep affection, because anger dissipates.

Another key characteristic of valuable emotions for the writer is the tendency to stimulate memory. Humans remember people and events that are tied to intense and lasting emotions. So characters, as well as the readers of the story, should experience significant, intense, credible, and memorable feelings that in some way change the character, or reader, in some irreversible, unforgettable way.

Chapter 3

How Literary Stories Go Wrong

Symptoms of unsuccessful literary stories.

1. *Failure to engage the reader*
2. *Too clever prose*
3. *Excessive and Static Details*
   Example 3: static and active description
4. *In-Your-Face Attitude.*
5. *Fatalism*
6. *Need to Shock*

How Literary Stories Go Wrong

In literary fiction the author creates, through imagination, a story that causes some enlightenment or change in thinking about the human condition and, if successful, this is unforgettable. For the reader, enjoyment comes from sympathizing with the character(s), sometimes without liking them, and finding satisfaction in realizing how character traits drive the plot progression.

In today's publishing environment, genre and commercial fiction survive. Literary fiction barely hangs on, but for a limited number of readers it is still the most enjoyable reading and it provides levels of satisfaction for them that commercial fiction cannot.

For the serious writer, literary fiction is not memoir, nor creative nonfiction, nor dependent on autobiographical material, although these techniques are commonly used and accepted in what is now published as primarily "non-genre", or mainstream, fiction. However, these techniques erode the imaginative decision process to choose the best action and details for characterization, and the most effective and credible motivation for plot energy. Devoted writers find literary fiction difficult to craft but representative of high achievement. When the characterization and the plot depend more on the reality of what has happened rather than on the imagination, the writer loses an artistic edge of excellence in his or her writing. Writers of mainstream fiction tend to depend on prose manipulation to write, and fail to grasp the advantage of well-imagined characters and plots motivated with innovative desires and frustrations.

Symptoms of unsuccessful literary stories

1. *Failure to engage the reader*

The most significant failure for a story is the inability of the reader to engage in the characters and the story. A good story engages the reader within the first few paragraphs. Without engagement, meaning for the story is lost, concentration is diverted, and enjoyment is minimal.

There are no formulas to assure reader engagement. The achievement is unique to each writer and reader, and does not occur with universal intensity. Still, every author must strive to engage the reader effectively and early.

2. *Too clever prose*

Great literary stories are a series of events with conflict and action that result in meaningful resolution through enlightenment or change in existing thought. The author achieves this through accurate word choice; logical thought progression; concrete, fresh images; and perfectly chosen, metaphoric enlightenments. Never is the story improved when accuracy, logic, freshness, or precise metaphors are compromised by the author slipping into clever prose (excessive lyricism, abstract ideas, cliches and phrases that are obscure and without clear modifiers). Of course, readers and editors seek and enjoy tastefully expansive prose, and lyrical prose can be beautiful in clear, image-filled, and significant ways. However, "too clever" prose is inflated, expanded, baroque, and directly opposed to succinct, purposeful story writing.

Clever prose is, of course, mostly a subject evaluation, but when prose becomes ineffective or irritating, it most often relates to overwriting with words unclear in meaning.

3. *Excessive and Static Details*

Setting is essential for story, but excessive description of setting is not. When description is excessive, it is almost always static.

Example 3: clarification of static description, compare A (static) and B (action):

A. Static.

The small, black bird with the brilliant, red wings and inquisitive, yellow eyes, perched on the white picket fence, just out of reach of the tabby colored cat with a scar on his leg and one eye half-closed and scarred from some fight long ago.

OR

B. Active

The red-winged blackbird glided in for a landing, and the battle-tested tabby cat leaped up, claws out, and caught only the edge of one of the bird's wings to scratch a feather loose that floated down to the garden path as the bird safely landed on the fence a few feet away.

Comment. Use of too many adjectives, adverbs, or extended and vague metaphorical comparisons, can deaden the desired effect of a story, and should be avoided.

4. *In-Your-Face Attitude.*

When characterization and plot motivation begin to fail to produce effective and meaningful stories, there is often a dependence on voice and a character's attitude to try to make the story stand out. The writing filters character thinking and speech through an in-your-face style, often counter to existing convention and authority, using confrontational — usually descriptive — narrative. Even when done well, the effect is limited. In literary fictional stories, characterization develops well when deeper character traits are dependent on action, response to events, and scene development. In-your-face narrative tends to be most useful in a character sketch, and is rarely useful to develop a character who acts with strong, credible motivations to drive the plot in significant ways—ways that are the skeletons of literary stories.

5. *Fatalism*

Fatalism means plot predictability. In fiction, predictability is what the reader of genre fiction expects. Murder, investigation, justice. Man woos reluctant woman; they fall in love. Terrorist threatens the White House; terrorist thwarted. In literary fiction, plots are character driven, that is, the plot's action results from the free will decision making process of the major characters. Rather than ferreting out a murderer, a reader learns motivations and desires (the how and why) that must be understandable and credible for the reader (the hard part). Life may seem—and could be—predestined and fatalistic. Fiction, however, moves ahead on the foundation of human foibles, and is exciting and unpredictable, with choices, and never predestined.

6. *Need to Shock*

Surprise is essential to good writing, but excessive shock in writing does not support the success of a good literary story. In the literary story, shocking situations may breach credibility and will often embrace cliché, with prose straining to evoke unearned emotions in the reader. The need for shock in a literary story means more lasting elements of fiction are usually not present.

Chapter 4

Character in Literary Fiction

1. Development.

2. Complexity.

3. Maximizing opportunities.

4. Misconceptions.

5. Significance.

6. Stereotypes.

7. Character in different types of writing.

8. Character and Plot.

Summary

Character in Literary Fiction

Characterization in literary fiction has special importance, and authors need to develop their own sense of responsibility for full and effective character development.

1. *Development.*

Character is everything in literary fiction and character relates to — but does not replace — plot, setting, or theme and meaning. Although characters are sometimes described as round or flat, every character in fiction must have complexities and uniqueness that may or may not be written on the page. A character that does not need to be fully presented for the story may appear two dimensional, but there should be three dimensions in the creator's mind. Full character development demonstrates that the author has thought about the story as a unit, and depth of understanding of all characters indicates that underlying motivations are reasonable, dialogue is believable, and logic of action is clear.

2. *Complexity.*

A unique, realistic character is the essence of great fictional stories. A well-formed character that is not stereotypical will be embraced by the reader, and the characters will drive the momentum of the plot. However, character creation in fiction is complex.

At the start of character development, there are no restrictions; a character emerges unencumbered. The character must be unique but remain believable and within the boundaries set by the suspension of disbelief all fiction requires. Although, in general, the character must not be stereotypical, the reader must feel comfortable with a character and feel some familiarity. As a memorable character develops, the reader becomes attached and admires the character in the same way that they would begin to like a new acquaintance as a friend. This reader attachment is often associated with liking the character, but liking is not absolutely necessary. Respect and/or admiration are also strong attachments for a reader to a character.

As the character emerges, authors choose imaginative attributes acceptable to readers in the evolvement of the story. Subsequently, during revision, scenes, thoughts, actions, conflicts, and motivations that do not contribute maximally to the characters engaging the reader and driving the plot forward are eliminated or changed.

3. *Maximizing opportunities.*

To create a character in a literary story, an author faces a limited number of things that the character can think or do. In a short story, even for the protagonist, there may be only ten to twenty key characterization opportunities, often fewer. In novels there are more, but still limited, opportunities, with a longer time line and a wider range of development from the direct story line.

How do authors take key opportunities and make the most of them? First, the actions and thoughts of characters must be reasonable for the story and for the sensibilities of the reader. The actions and thoughts of characters must also be unique, with elements of surprise, so that the actions and traits are embedded in readers' memories. In-scene showing of a character's actions, thoughts, and opinions has more lasting impact than narrative telling. Character development leaves more of an impression on the reader when in-scene story time predominates, rather than with back story or comments on past character action by the narrator.

4. *Misconceptions.*

Two common ideas that lead to failed stories:
    1. Character sketches can substitute for a structured, well-written literary story.
    2. Detailed description of a character's action taken from a real life event of the author without fictionalization is acceptable for the literary story.

Character development by an author is not a specific or inherited, authorial trait. Authors learn and experience character development to improve their stories, and characters should never take over the author's creative responsibility in stories. Some authors credit an achievement of existential transcendence to their best writing trances; and, in the privacy of these trances, the character takes over to tell the story to completion. These authors are sincere, and at times successful in publication, but they have bypassed the concrete control an author needs to create a literary story as an art form. Characters are imagined and created—not discovered, absorbed, and described—for maximum story effectiveness.

5. *Significance.*

Stories, to be great, should be significant and meaningful. Significance in storytelling is achieved through effective characterization. Every significant character will have some heroic qualities and display courage against the obstacles faced. That, in varying degrees, is part of what every reader desires in stories. Authors must not be trivial, and must not write to bore the reader. Significance, not overdone, is essential to the good story.

6. *Stereotypes.*

A stereotypical (oversimplified, standardized image or idea) character is avoided in literary stories. But in fact, stereotypes are found in many stories, and are often essential in genre fiction. Comic super-heroes are so rigid that cartoonists must adhere strictly to the visual and story history already familiar to the reader; for example, consider *Spiderman*. In detective fiction, Hercules Perot, Agatha Christie's detective, is consistent crime after crime. He has a role that defines him and that is required for the story telling as she created it.

In literary fiction, every character is, by nature of the creative process, born stereotypical and then developed to some non-stereotypical threshold. This improves reader interest, and augments the quality of the story. However, in stories with multiple characters, all characters cannot be unique, vibrant, or memorable, and some stereotypes are unavoidable. This is not detrimental. Over-development of too many characters may create unbelievable and/or ineffective fiction. As in the writing of all fiction, proper balance must be sought.

7. *Character in different types of writing.*

Although many would reflexively disagree, it is true that memoir, creative nonfiction, and biography do not have the options and do not reach the potential of character development available to the fiction writer. Yet, much, if not the vast majority, of published fiction stories today are simply authors describing events that have happened, often to them or someone they know, with a little freedom from reality, calling the result fiction. A character and his or her traits are described. This result does not have the imaginative structure of fiction, and relies on narrative telling to the reader rather than in-scene engagement through action.

Nonfiction is also an easier venue for the lyrical writer — the poet of prose — to experiment with language. This is not all bad and is very enjoyable to some readers, but it does not address how to create great fictional stories. In fiction, characters emerge, plots progress, meanings arise, and structure supports a story created in the imagination and then skillfully crafted to provide entertainment for the reader. In contrast, in memoir the author is the character and the valuable differences between author, narrator, and character that exist in fiction are lost. Fiction demands that readers know more than the characters, and often more than the narrator. Fiction is not as reliant on the discovery of something already known, but rather on the awareness of how and why something happens based on character and plot.

In biography and autobiography, the character is formed before the writing starts. The author chooses accurate descriptions of happenings. There are few decisions allowing change for the betterment of the story. In fiction, a character is formed to function in the reality of the story world.

8. *Character and Plot.*

In literary fiction, characters move the plot. Consider some brief plot descriptions:

1. The plane crashed.
2. The drunken pilot crashed in a stolen plane.
3. The grief-stricken pilot, rejected by his second wife, fails to listen to a transmission from the tower and is injured after a midair collision.
4. The plane was shot down by enemy fire.
5. The nearly bankrupt airline failed to pay maintenance man Joe Hubbard for two months and Joe refused to perform a routine maintenance check; yet Max Fine, the supervisor, allowed the plane to fly and the plane crashed.

These scenarios demonstrate how plot can be circumstantial (1 and 4) or character motivated (2, 3 and 5). These are not suggested as worthy of development.

Summary

The author who wants to create great stories must characterize well. Time and multiple tries are required, and a healthy dissatisfaction with all early opportunities is essential. In fact, during the creative process, authors must continue to search for improved characterization, never being satisfied with mediocrity.

Chapter 5

Credibility in Literary Fiction

Credibility in Literary Fiction

There is a tendency for an author to dismiss consideration of credibility, often in an attempt to be unique and original. However, authors must address credibility issues; successful stories depend on credible plots, characters, narrators, and settings, and on credible desires and motivations.

Credibility (willingness to accept something as true in the characters and in their story world) must be meticulously nurtured in the literary story as an art form. Often, credibility slips with illogical progression of plot ideas, or with poorly integrated character thoughts, actions, and words. Readers will fail to connect to a story where there is erosion of credibility, and the writing will not succeed. Even if the story requires suspension of disbelief – as all stories do to some degree – there is always a dependency on the absolutely logical association and progression of ideas.

Credibility in plot logic is the easiest to identify and discuss. As characters move through the story, choices are made for their action in the plot. Lazy or untalented choices will sink the story. For example, a prodigal son comes to the bedside of his dying father, whom he has not seen since childhood. What happens next? Some possibilities: He falls on his knees and weeps. He smothers his father to death with a pillow. He asks his sister to bring him a drink. He remains motionless, unable to feel emotion. The smell of his father's breath forces memories of childhood abuse. And so forth. There are so many choices, but there is only one right choice for any one great story. The choice must be the most credible choice, the one that fits without a ripple between what has happened and what will happen. That doesn't mean to abandon surprise, or reversal, or enlightenment, or any change, it just means that what happens must be believable. An author finds that best choice after he or she seeks alternative after alternative. Most of these choices are made in the mind, but often an outline helps for timing and positioning, especially with critical story actions. Never take your first thought as your best, it rarely will be.

You may think of credibility issues on two levels. First, the immediate: Are immediate story action and thoughts, reflections, or words of a character logical for that moment and for what the reader knows about that character at that moment? Second, overall: Is the character developing in the story logically and along lines closely related to the theme of the story? Characters are chosen for a story by authors for (1) the capabilities of either having significant enlightenment about something or (2) for their potential to have significant changes in their thinking and beliefs about something. As characters are developed, details and actions must be logical for how the characters will be irreversibly changed.

Credible emotional content in a scene must also be considered to match exactly what is needed for the story for the moment. Paradoxically, to create tension in the reader from emotions in the story, it is not sufficient to crank up the language with four letter expletives, two-word sentences and imperatives, and describe things as brightest and loudest. In fact, in the best writing, worthy emotional scenes are created without emotionally charged, abstract language ("He was flooded by fear and love" is not effective writing), but by terse, clear, concrete language and structure. The emotional valence of a scene must also coincide with what the reader will expect at any point in the story. Surprise is also a necessary component in story telling, but the surprise must be credible, too. To fail breaks the connection between reader and character that is necessary for good stories.

It may seem odd, but credibility need not relate to the reality of the reader's world. Credibility is judged by the story world created by the author and told by the narrator. So a plot shift or a character decision set in 1929 only needs to be credible for the story, and does not need to be credible for the reader's time in existence, although at times it may be necessary. As the story is introduced, there is a contract of details established between the author and readers – unstated of course – that continues to develop throughout the story and that will establish what is and is not credible.

In *summary*: for credibility, the final fictional story product, novel or short story, must have reasonable thoughts and actions built on logical associations and progressions, total reader acceptance of timing and progression of story elements, and total believability that the emotional content of the writing matches the need for story development.

Chapter 6

1st person POV in Literary Story

I. *Mastering 1st person point of view*

    Advantages

    Disadvantages

    Example 4: POV

II. *Using 1st person POV*

    Example 5: multiple POVs

III. *Distance in 1st person POV: psychic and physical*

IV. *Awkward Constructions in 1st person*

V. *Feelings, drama, and structure*

VI. *Narrator and "I" character*

    Example 6: extraneous thought

    Example 7: same scene with different POVs

VII. *Present tense and 1st person POV*

1st person POV in Literary Story

Purpose: to explore character development when using 1st person point of view in literary storytelling.

Many fiction writers are successful in publication without exploring the intricacies of 1st person POV. To achieve high character development for the great story that has a character based plot, authors can improve their writing by understanding how characters affect readers, and then apply the effects through controlled writing. Authorial control of point of view, especially in 1st person, where options are limited, is a key way to heighten reader emotions.

Terminology:

> *POV = point of view.
> *1st person refers to "I" pronoun usage in a prose story, but the "I" character may not be the protagonist or even a major character.

I. *Mastering 1st person point of view.*

1st person POV use is effective when the author chooses this point of view for the right reasons. For the author of literary fiction, the choice must assure best story telling so the reader is involved with the character. Consider that in the 1st person point of view the following disadvantages and advantages are in play. Advantages and disadvantages will vary in importance according to the story structure and content, and, of course, with the abilities of the author.

Advantages of 1st person

> 1) In narrative telling of the story to the reader, 1st person POV provides the sense of having been there with the action (or being there, in the present tense), and adds a memoir quality of telling my story as the straight scoop to you, the reader. There is a psychic and physical closeness to the action that provokes intimacy.

2) 1st person POV gives the reader constant characterization; that is, the thoughts and actions of the "I" character. All other characters, even if the protagonist is not the "I" character, are secondary because of limited access to their thoughts and actions. This consistent access to one character's opinions and attitudes often strengthens voice, and allows easier access to sarcasm, cynicism, and injection of surprise-humor.

3) The 1st person POV flows more easily into an intuitive writing style, giving a certain freedom from the necessity of structure.

Disadvantages of 1st person

1) In 1st person, the acceptance of a character's dialog changes. In 1st person POV dialog, the reader knows any character's dialogue other than the 1st person is actually being presented, and might be altered in tone and credibility, by the 1st person. Some themes and meanings require reliability on the integrity of character dialog to reach meaningful impact on the reader. A 1st person character that is unreliable tends to confuse the reader as to what and who to believe in a story (often referred to as unreliable narrator—a loosely defined term). In character-based fiction this may work against the significance and the perfection of the story.

Example 4: POV

1st Person

      We were standing at the edge of the thousand foot drop on Mount Hood. Carol shivered and looked away from me. "I'd like to shove your ass into eternity," she said. I smiled. "I'm not joking," she said.

Comment. In the 1st person POV presentation, we do not know what Carol really said, or meant, in the story world; we know only what the 1st person POV told us she said and how she spoke. In third person presentation, through a narrator or a character, the reader may interpret Carol's words differently, and with an interpretation specific to each reader that will affect the story differently.

3rd person

At the precipice, Paul looked down a thousand feet to the snow covered rocks below. Carol stared at the side of his head, her fists clenched.

"I'd like to shove your ass into eternity," she said.

He expected warmth but her gaze made him unsure what to think.

He smiled.

"I'm not joking," she said. The arrogant bastard. She knew exactly what she had to do.

Comment. There are many ways to structure this mini-scene, but the examples show how Carol's words can be interpreted differently in multiple points of view. At times, a scene can be given more impact by not filtering all information through the single conduit of the "I" character.

2) The 1st person POV limits knowing what other characters feel and think, characters that may have a more informed view of the story world and may be better sources of significant contribution to conflict and action.

3) Because of limitation mainly to the mind of the "I" character, the reader has no comparative gauge to test the credibility of the "I" character's view of the world, accuracy of story presentation, or validity of opinions and conclusions. Credibility in storytelling is a fragile, at times abstract, phenomenon that when highly developed may allow significant impact of story meaning. With a lack of credibility in character, plot, and/or story world perceptions, the chances for a great story are often lost.

4) In 1st person POV, easy access to distance from the action is lost.

II. *Using 1st person POV*

How comfortable the use of a single character in the 1st person POV is for an author. How easy the telling is.

I was sitting at this gay bar studded with full-sized Michelangelo statues of David at each end, and this girl couple walks in, one ugly, but the other one so gorgeous she made my heart throb. In a split second, I was falling in love with a dyke, and I hadn't even thrown back a gulp of my straight up Port Ellen.

The mood is chatty with attitude, a story that will be interpreted entirely through a character who provides the reader with the only his/her opinions, thoughts, and abilities to observe and articulate the story.

The first person character shades, changes, and filters reality. If the story progression and meaning depend on the belief that the POV character is presenting reality, the use of 1st person POV may inhibit the creation of a great story. A reader's belief that characters' situations are real, or could be real, often enhances the reader's engagement and emotional response in a story. Story writing improves when an author is aware, and in control, of the perception of reality in the story. And this story type will often rely on the ironies created by the differences between the "I" persona and how he or she perceives his or her world.

There are many flexible approaches to the use of 1st person POV. This story could be altered to include more in-scene delivery, which would result in seemingly more objective story information, and a change of attitude.

> My heart pounded when I saw a five-foot-two blond with her girlfriend. She walked with confidence, her short shorts creasing the flesh of her thigh as she moved. She smiled and looked away. I gulped my scotch and wondered if she could switch-hit the way I was imagining.

This moving in scene, rather than a narrative telling, sets a different tone, and is more action oriented. Now compare a 3rd person (multi-character plus narrator) delivery (not to be labeled as omniscient).

> Jared sat on a red Naugahyde barstool with his foot on a brass rail, close enough to touch the life-sized statue of Michelangelo's David that stood at bar's end as decoration. He'd wanted Johnny Walker Black but the bartender had quotas to meet by serving the most expensive drink possible and Jared had wound up with Port Ellen scotch. That didn't do much for his sour mood. When Doris entered with Camille, their arms linked to express their attachment, Jared's gaze turned to Doris, and she smiled, not sure if

he realized that the obvious desire he couldn't hide would never be satisfied.

Note how information is presented with possible consciousness of multiple characters and the narrator.

Example 5: multiple POVs

Key: identifying the shifts in POV
Narrator or protagonist providing information (POV).
Protagonist (character) information (POV).
Bartender (minor character) information (POV).
<u>Doris's, and possibly Camille's, information (POV).</u>

Jared sat on a red Naugahyde barstool with his foot on a brass rail, close enough to touch the life-sized statue of Michelangelo's David that stood at bar's end as decoration. *He'd wanted Johnny Walker Black* but **the bartender had quotas to meet by serving the most expensive drink possible** and Jared had wound up with Port Ellen scotch. *That didn't do much for his sour mood.* When Doris entered with Camille, <u>their arms linked to express their attachment</u>, Jared's gaze turned to Doris, and she smiled, <u>not sure if he realized that the obvious desire he couldn't hide would never be satisfied.</u>

Skeptics can reasonably argue that the these complexities of point of view are artificially micromanaged, and that authors should do what feels right and is effective for their purpose in their writing. That is the essence of style one might point out. Yet, in literary fiction, an author is trying to intensely engage the reader and provide lasting and significant insight to the reader with ideas never before considered, or pleasingly revisited. For success, expert characterization and a character driven plot are necessary, and the more control the author has of the writing, and of the story telling, the better chance for creating a lasting, enjoyable, and significant story. Understanding POV clearly, and knowing the potential of efficient POV usage, helps authors write their best stories.

III. *Distance in 1st person POV: psychic and physical.*

1) Psychic distance vaguely means how emotionally involved the character is in the action. It is internal. In psychic distance, the single 1st person POV limits breadth of emotional development and restricts one character to a "tight" range of reaction. When story presentation allows character distance, aspects of reasonable and objective information about character, plot and meaning are often enhanced. Psychic distance is more easily created in third person, with one or more points of view.

2) Physical distance is the distance the character is from the action. It is external. Physical distance allows more expansive imagery and broader interpretations. Different possibilities exist between a 1st person POV plunging to almost certain death in seat number 24C in an airplane while telling or showing the pre-death moment and a narrator who describes (even in-scene), after the fact, the same disaster by telling or showing the character from a later point in time than depicted in the story, and being able to imagine, and feel, from yards, miles, or eons away from the action. More objectivity becomes possible, albeit with a loss of immediacy.

IV. *Awkward Constructions in 1ˢᵗ person*

The effects of 1st person POV storytelling are distinctly different, and somewhat more restrictive, than other narrative techniques, and, as previously mentioned, 1st person POV is often chosen by beginning writers because the style is intuitively easier to write. Also, there is an immediacy and intensity effect, a sort of whisper-in-our-ear phenomenon, which provides an intimacy between narrator and reader. Problems do exist, however. The 1st person POV has difficulty credibly expressing the feelings of others, or out of scene action that is necessary to the story. These problems may make for awkward prose.

> Examples of awkward constructions in 1st person created when the author must filter information through the "I" 1ˢᵗ person character.

>> 1) From the fire in her eyes, I knew exactly how she felt — enraged and hurt, and probably a little embarrassed, too.

>>> (Compare: Her eyes burned with anger as she lowered her head and cried, her face red with embarrassment.)

>> 2) In the dressing room, I knew the Hardrocks were tuning up, their grimy hands turning the geared pegs, the strings whining with tension.

>>> (Compare: The Hardrocks tuned their guitars, their grimy hands twisting pegs. The strings whined.)

V. *Feelings, drama, and structure*

1) 1st person POV can be the perfect way to achieve a great literary story. However, one barrier is the way feelings are delivered to the reader. When authors find 1st person POV comfortable, they tend to tell real or imagined events that have made them feel a certain

way, but telling feelings does not have the same impact on readers as showing how feelings develop through action.

2) Great stories enlighten or reverse thinking about something. They have theme and purpose. To reach maximum potential, stories must be structured for purposeful delivery through dramatic events. Writers must have a clear understanding about how the story is narrated, with elements of narrator reliability and clear moral thermometer readings, logical motivation reasonably tied to all other action and motivations in the story, and dedication to story purpose rather than author performance.

3) Writing in 1st person POV makes the delivery of the story seem easier. There are certain shared attitudes with the reader that can easily bring a sympathetic response, and it is easier to tell feelings, rather than illustrate them through action.

4) 1st person may seduce an author into making intuitive decisions about the story structure that may not be appropriate choices for the best story and the management of emotional responses.

VI. *Narrator and "I" character*

In storytelling, an author creates, a narrator tells, and a character acts. It is usually more prudent not to alter this in 1st person by collapsing the author into the character to narrate the story. Narrators provide crucial and truthful information, and are necessary in almost every story; though narrative information delivered by a 1st person character may be awkward, or unbelievable. For great stories, the narrator also has to be more knowledgeable about the the story world than the character, even in 1st person POV. Many 1st person stories simple use the 1st POV to surreptitiously provide narrator information, but this can lead to disbelief and mistrust of the character that in turn leads to a feeling of artificiality in the storytelling.

Authors can't always resist interjecting their own opinions and attitudes into the story world. This can be as subtle as a single adverb or it can involve the use of phrases, clauses, and sentences.

> **Example 6**: extraneous thought
>
> She was killing him. He would have no water, and he would die of thirst. The idea pleased her. She held a glass before him, and tipped it onto the floor, ignoring the draught that had raged in the city from the effects of global warning.

Extraneous thoughts, no matter how important, can push the reader away from the story.

In general, narrators should be more objective and reliable than characters, so in the 1st person POV, narrator presence may be needed when objectivity and reliability are important for clarity and story purpose.

When an author becomes the narrator, there tends to be a blurring, or confusion, of the telling time. In storytelling, the real time of writing and the narrator's time of telling can effectively be different, and these may be different from the story's action time. This may allow irony and justify cynicism. An author writing in March of 2008 may do well having a narrator, even in 1st person, tell the story from the time of 1875 about a character acting the story out as in 1st person POV in 1862. The differences, however, need not be years, but may be weeks, or days, or fractions of an hour.

Example 7: same scene with different POVs

Example 7A.

> There was no doubt the ship was sinking. The captain sat alone, stone faced, in his cabin; his illustrious career turned infamous in minutes. In the radio room, the operator had twisted the knob off the now silent radio and laid his head on his arms. Below deck, the engineer failed to seal a compartment door and a rush of water banged his head on a girder, causing him to lose consciousness before he drowned.
>
> I watched as the lifeboat hit the water and rocked violently for a few seconds. Someone pushed me from behind.
>
> "Dear, God," I said. I jumped over the rail toward the boat thirty feet below and felt my lower leg crack as I hit one of the wooden seats that broke my fall.
>
> "Move out of the way," someone said, kicking me in the ribs.

Comment. Many readers (and writing instructors) would not accept this construction in 1st person. However, when successfully used, narrator information can be presented to enhance story movement and understanding. A narrator provides information the 1st person cannot know at the time of delivering his specific information. For many readers—who serve as POV police—any deviation from a 1st person POV is an error, or at least a slippage in writing skills. Here is what might be suggested, or required, in revision. In this example, dialogue is used to deliver story information within the 1st person POV.

Example 7B.

We were crowded near the railing on the port side, with the deck slanting twenty degrees. "The Captain's taken to his cabin. He ain't seeing no visitors," a man said.

"Career ruined," a sailor said.

"A dead man," said another.

"The radio's out."

"The engine room flooded a few minutes ago. I saw the engineer floating face down with my own eyes."

Someone pushed me from behind. I looked down to the lifeboat as it hit the water and rocked. A deck officer shoved me. Three of us fell at the same time. My leg cracked as I hit the edge of a wooden seat. Pain seared upward. Someone kicked me in the ribs.

"Get out of the way," he said.

Comment. For many, this attempt to provide information through dialogue is awkward. A major distraction is that the dialogue is delivered as the speakers are facing death, and it has a barroom chatty tone (this is exposition mistakenly filtered through dialogue) and rings with a lack of credibility and therefore makes the scene seem less real and harder to accept and enjoy.

The information might be provided through internal reflection.

Example 7C.

I imagined the Captain alone in his cabin, a man with a stellar career ruined. I doubted the distress signals were going out anymore. The silent bridge was eerie among the yells and shouts on the deck. A man said the forward compartment had flooded, and he thought he heard the cries of the engineer who suddenly became silent. The lifeboat dropped, the winch handle spinning to a blur. Someone pushed me and I fell, hitting the gunnels. My leg cracked and a searing pain shot upward in me. Someone kicked me in the ribs to move me out of the way to clear space for others to fall.

Comment. But that seems awkward, too. Another try that is much more internal:

Example 7D.

> With the deck slanting, I could not stand without gripping a rope or a metal ring fixed to flooring. My fall had broken my leg above the knee; pain seared through me with every movement. But I held on, waiting for the cries to signal when a rescue boat might be below. I was close enough to the rail to be in the crowd that would jump the twenty feet below the slanting deck.
>
> "I can't jump," a woman whispered to me, sobbing, clutching my leg to keep from slipping violently into the rail. I yelled out in pain. Was she an evil woman? Did she deserve to die? There was no time to lower her into a boat securely and safely. She'd have to jump. She'd have to be forced. Was there someone to do it? Even with my leg whole, I could never shove a woman, or any human, to possible death. She had to make that decision, not me.
>
> "Do you have family?" I asked. That brought more sobs and she did not answer. The ship's horn blasted. The passengers panicked and began to jump. A few hit the boat, but most went into the water, looking for something to cling to, a deck chair, an oar, some piece of ocean debris. They'd all be unconscious in two to three minutes, motionless with the cold, clumped with broken ice.
>
> I began to pray.

There is no right way, and when solutions don't readily come up, 3rd person or narrator POV presentations might be considered. To change a POV is a drastic undertaking, and an even more crucial question might be asked: Are the information and the scene necessary? Is it time to delete this scene?

Most successful authors don't consider alternatives, or narrator based information, in a 1st person POV delivered story. They go with the gut feeling of what works, and that usually results in the author and character being inseparable—and it tilts toward writing memoir and losing many advantages of good fiction. However, ignoring narrator function is not the right attitude for creating the great literary story.

VII. *Present tense and 1st person POV.*

In any presentation (point of view), a story is told from a point in time, related to the existence of the author and the reader. This can be thought of as the period in which the story is set. Many writers loosely assume that this time is clear when using the 1st person POV because the writer creates the story as if it is occurring at the time of the writing, or at a consistent time in the past.

In truth, all stories have happened. No one reading a story actually lives the story, either at the time the story is created or at the time the story is supposed to happen. At times, present tense is used to create a sense that the story is happening now. This is, of course, a deception — an often acceptable and effective deception, but still not a reality. Verbs indicating present action require suspension of disbelief that the story is happening now. The attempted deception of immediacy can complicate effective, in-depth characterization, and confuse back story and front story. When a story is in past tense, the timeline is easier to establish and convey to the reader.

The pleasing effects of 1st person immediacy and strong voice may become tiresome at times, and adding the inherent deception of present tense may work against reader enjoyment of a story. Still, both present tense and 1st person serve important roles in every writer's choices.

Chapter 7

Narration of Literary Stories

Definitions

1. *In-scene vs. narrative telling.*

2. *Point of view.*

     Example 8: point of view.

3. *Voice.*

4. *Principles of narration.*

5. *Thinking of oral story tradition when writing.*

6. *Terms.*

     Narrator intrusion

     Authorial intrusion

     1st person point of view is the same as the narrator

     Close (or tight) vs. distant character points of view

     Narrator point of view

     Omniscient narrator

     Omniscient author

     Story world

     Narrator epiphany

     Time line and point of view

     Multiple 3rd person

     Suspension of Disbelief

Narration of Literary Stories

Authors who continue to refine their thinking about narration improve the quality of their stories. Clear authorial thinking about story information presented to the reader, and knowing how narrator and character functions interact best, improves both characterization and story effect.

Definitions

> To learn the skill of narrating a story in fiction, authors, teachers, and students must know what words mean and not confuse terms or use them interchangeably. Note, in particular, the difference in the meanings of narrative the noun and narrative the adjective, narrator and character, and literary fiction and memoir.

*Narrate, v: to give an account of something in detail.

*Narrator, n: somebody who tells a story or gives an account of something.

*Character, n: one of the people portrayed in a story.

*Narration, n: the act of telling a story or giving an account of something.

*Narrative, n: an account of a sequence of events in the order in which they happened.

*Narrative, adj: having aim or purpose of telling a story, or involving the art of story telling.

*Author, n: the creator or originator of something.

*Fiction: stories that describe imaginary people and events.

*Literary fiction: serious, character-based fiction as opposed to genre or popular fiction, which are plot based.

*Story: an account of a series of events.

*Memoir: an account of events written from personal knowledge.

*Autobiography: an account of someone's life written by that person.

*Biography: an account of someone's life written by another person.

*Creative nonfiction: literary or narrative journalism, using literary skills in writing nonfiction.

1. *In-scene vs. narrative telling.*

Authors must clarify their own thinking about how to provide story information: 1) story advanced by telling a sequence of events, 2) in-scene reader involvement by showing character action in events.

Show-don't-tell has been the imperative in literary fiction for centuries, but increasingly fewer authors respond. The result is fewer good stories created as an art form.

2. *Point of view.*

Character points of view are used by a narrator to tell a story. First person and third person are most commonly used. (Second person is trendy but rarely provides the lasting reader satisfaction necessary for great storytelling.) The narrator has a point of view that may be used for improving time management of story progression or for information that is not within the reasonable range of the character's senses, memory (life experiences), education, or intelligence.

Point of view has many definitions. Most commonly, writers think of point of view as 1) a position in space, time, or development from which something is considered. Point of view can also be 2) a manner of evaluating something, or 3) a reasoned opinion about something. In essence, a character point of view is not simply a position for considering physical action in a story. It is a character-revealing way for the narrator to present story information to the reader. There are complexities of point of view that, if not appreciated or if mismanaged, will cause the reader to unnecessarily question the character's reliability —and withhold sympathetic judgments.

(It is not helpful to think of a point of view in story telling as a camera, as is often taught. Evaluating story action and opinions are also involved, things a camera does not do. This broad approach to point of view is especially useful when considering use of narrator and character points of view together.)

> **Example 8:** point of view.
>
> I despised Amy. She was beautiful, I'll give her that, but she thought the world revolved around her – that God made her for other people to admire. Never once did she think of me, or anyone, as a human with feelings.

Comment. The structure of this paragraph is common and acceptable to many readers. Yet it has a complexity of point of view that requires a reader to suspend disbelief in the character's capabilities. In essence, telling what Amy thought and wanted is not within reasonable boundaries of the 1st person point of view. However, it is necessary information, which is best thought of as narrator information since a narrator knows all about the story world and has the reader-acceptable gift of knowing what all characters think.

Information provided through a character, first or third person, that is not reasonable makes that character unreliable, either intentionally or unintentionally. A character does not know the truth of Amy's thoughts, and also shows arrogance in telling the reader these impossibilities. These may not be aspects of the character the author always wants to imply. However, it is perfectly reasonable, and often necessary, to use a first person character as the more story story-wise narrator. However, it must not be accidental, and it must be consistent for the story being written.

Resist thinking that unraveling complexities of point of view is unnecessary, the if-it-works-and-I wrote-it, it-must-be-good approach to creating fictional stories. Authors must be aware of the subtle and complex layers of point of view so that they can use point of view effectively. It is inescapable. Well-reasoned opinions about point of view are essential for all authors who want to be in control of the storytelling process and what they provide for a reader.

3. *Voice.*

Voice and point of view, although related, must not be equated. Voice is everything a character does and says that helps identify the character. Point of view is how story information is presented, and can be thought of as microscopic (close) or telescopic (distant). While characters deliver story information in their own voice, a narrator is telling the story that is specific to the narrator—even in first person.

4. *Principles of narration.*

A. Great stories are told by a narrator, not by a character.

B. Narration of a story and point of view are separate, and the narrator uses a point of view to deliver the story. (When done seamlessly, the reader becomes engrossed and does not register how the narrator is delivering story information, either directly or through a character. A narrator is present both in first person or third person points of view, although the narrator may be more submerged and unrecognizable in 1st person point of view.)

C. A narrator is created by an author but should be thought of as a distinct intellect who is telling the story.

5. *Thinking of oral story tradition when writing.*

In academic discussions and workshops, terms are frequently used without common understanding as to their meaning. It is a practice that has resulted in entire careers riddled with confusions about the basics of storytelling and the unique problems in the written story.

It is often helpful, in discussions of point of view and narrators, to think of an oral story telling tradition. The storyteller is always telling the story, and the teller is often not the author of the story and is in control of narrative passages, action, dialog, and internal reflection. At times, the storyteller relies on suspension of disbelief that the storyteller could know the information presented to increase tension and infuse drama. Listeners can have transcendence as if they were within the character's living self.

Imagine Ornesto, a storyteller, telling Henry James's story, "Turn of the Screw," in 2008 to a high school literature class. James published "Turn of the Screw" in 1898. Ornesto, to be effective in his dramatization, will make the presentation as familiar to his contemporary (2008) audience as possible. Ornesto's storytelling will be affected by his generation: stories told by tellers born in 1972 are different from those told by those born in 1938. Moreover, the author's generation is in the previous century. All this has an effect on the story told.

Ornesto, telling a story already open to decades of interpretations, will tell it in his way, in 2008. He might dip into Flora's or Mile's minds, choosing the most relevant facts for his purpose, or characterize Mrs. Grose with room left for the 2008 listeners to fill in their own details. Ornesto will make Peter Quint as evil as he can, choosing his words (mostly, if not all, from James) for best effect. Ornesto is the narrator—knowing all about the story world, and choosing story facts from a limited story-world perspective. (James is considered the creator of the story world with knowledge outside the story world.)

Note that as narrator, Ornesto will make the best choices about story information for his audience. It is this separation-advantage of author from narrator from character(s) that fiction writers often ignore. Now Ornesto, to keep his story moving, will narrate, and may use different points of view, other than what Henry James would, to be effective.

Here is a useful rule: although the fiction author writes the story, the author should not tell the story. The narrator tells the story (that is created by the author) and moves within the limits of the story world. The narrator uses the narrator's voice for certain story information, and uses character point(s) of view to deliver other story content. This prevents stray ideas of the author from entering into the story, keeps the story focused, forces more consistent voices, and intensifies the effect of the writing on the reader.

There are two difficult concepts to digest: 1) by clear conceptualization of author-narrator-character delivered information, authors add ease to reader understanding, and 2) when contemporary writers choose a single character's point of view exclusively as if it were a selective filter, they often limit the potential of the story.

6. *Terms.*

Narrator intrusion

Narrators contribute to the story presentation and direct decisions about character contribution. To call a narrator's contribution to the story an intrusion is usually a result of poor writing, but good judgment is necessary. If narrator information does not fit into the continuous fictional dream of the story provided for the reader at that moment, it is an intrusion and should not be included. Authors must use narrative techniques while remaining true to quality storytelling.

Authorial intrusion

Any thought, opinion, or emotion of the author in a story should be removed as detrimental to creating a story as an art form. Most common are political ideas or needs to comment on real world social change. (The story may deal with these issues, but through action enlightenment, not narrative emotional descriptions.) Author intrusion often borders on essay and propaganda and is not compatible with great stories.

(This does not mean that themes and meaning important to the author are not an integral part of great stories. They are, but they are expressed through careful story structure and skillful, craft-savvy presentation.)

It is important that the authorial morality be understood and be consistent. All good literary stories are constructed on a moral framework that is easily perceived by the reader. Moral fiction is the cardiovascular system of a literary fictional story, and is provided by the author as a matrix in which the characters and narrator act.

1st person point of view is the same as the narrator

When the narrator collapses into the first person character, although it seems logical and acceptable, it often sets up unaddressed, but perceived, questions in the reader's mind as to who is telling the story.

Close (or tight) vs. distant character points of view

The reader's sense of how close the character is to the story action is created by syntax, word choice, and ideation. This is true in all choices for story, including presentation, dialog, narration, description, internal reflection, and even exposition. As a character seems more distant from the action, they function more and more as a narrator. The author who recognizes character and narrator information in close and distant terms is able to present more consistent voicings, more in-depth character reliability, easier grasped imagery, and will be in better control of the writing process.

In essence, use of narrator information (that is, information not filtered through a character's point of view) provides flexibility to provide essential story information that is outside the senses, knowledge, and/or intellectual capabilities of the character. This is useful technique in all but the rare story.

Narrator point of view

The narrator point of view is not a silo in a field of character point of view silos. Narrators tell stories, and it is not useful to consider a narrator's point of view as similar or equivalent to a character's point of view. Narrators float above the story in a hot air balloon, with useful overviews that characters cannot achieve.

Omniscient narrator (Omniscient: knowing everything.)

Narrators only know about their story worlds. That is their *raison d'être*. They know more than is told in the story but they do not know all that the author knows and they should not tell what the author knows and believes outside the story world. This is an important distinction for an author who wants to tell stories effectively.

Omniscient author

This implies the author knows all truths. Impossible. Authors know only what they perceive of their world, and it is never omniscient. Omniscience is reserved for deities.

Story world

Story world is restricted, selective, purposeful, intense, directed, and never random. It is where the characters act and it is what the narrator delivers to the reader. In good fiction, its boundaries are sacrosanct and should not be violated.

Narrator epiphany

In general, narrators tell stories and may or may not change. Usually, characters change from revelations or changes in the way they think about something brought about by story action. However, there are many exceptions. Many stories have very effective narrators blessed with revelations and reversal in thinking that may or may not be similar to a character. Note also that when the author is considered to be equal to the narrator, the narrator's enlightenment is awkward if not impossible. How characters, and sometimes narrators, change in a story needs to be under the author's control.

Time line and point of view

A character's point of view changes with the advancement of the story time. (There are three elements of point of view, all of which are a part of our understanding of point of view: position in space or time, a mental attitude or opinion, and a manner of evaluating.)

Multiple 3rd person points of view equals omniscient point of view

Points of view in a story are not spices in a stew that give a blended effect. Points of view are pears, figs, cashews, and marshmallows, all in a bowl that are consumed separately with sometimes memorable and always distinct individual effects that contribute to the whole experience of eating. Omniscient point of view is not equal to multiple points of view, and its use in discussion of point of view is not helpful.

Suspension of Disbelief

Characters and situations can often be believed to be real. For a reader, sympathizing with a possibly real character is easier and often more intense. However, all fiction requires a reader to say: to enjoy this story, I am willing to not think about (suspend) characters and situations that I know could never exist and never be real. Some readers are more tolerant than others. To feel emotional responses to the plights of Batman or Superman requires considerable suspension of what might be real. For writers seeking the maximum effects of their literary fiction, the degree of suspension-of-disbelief required of their readers is an important consideration. In general, a sense of reality will enhance a reader's genuine engagement and validate their emotional responses. Writer's work on this truth: readers wish they were characters because they want to experience what the character would experience if that character did exist. So perceptions of reality are important.

Chapter 8

Information and literary story structure

1. *Story information: is it true to the story?*

2. *Story information: hold or reveal.*

3. *Omniscience and point of view.*

4. *Dos and don'ts.*

Information and literary story structure

Every fictional story is composed of information selected from an infinite number of imagined possibilities. Once the information to be used has been selected, almost invariably requiring drafts and outlines, then the process of revision should include the consideration of story information: is it essential to the story? Is it in the right place? Is it clear? Is it used to provide an effect on the readers or to guide them through a story?

As each of these questions is addressed, often simultaneously, in the author's revision process, the author has to begin to look at information to create suspense in the reader (What is it? Why did it happen? Who was it? How did it happen? Where did it happen?). The literary story differs from a genre story in the way information is presented to the reader and the knowledge known about the story by the characters and narrator in comparison to what the reader and author knows.

1. Story information: is it true to the story?

Authors often write about what is important to them. It's natural. However, even well-written, important information that is not directly related to story characterization or plot movement will deaden the effect of story meaning and enjoyment for the reader.

2. Story information: hold or reveal.

In a literary story, information withheld is not the same as information withheld in a genre story for commercial fiction. In a mystery, for example, the reader wants to guess who committed the murder, and the author presents many possibilities and tries to allow reasonable surprise when the murderer is revealed. In suspense and thriller writing, the reader seeks to see what happened, and cares about characters so tension is built when what happened is withheld until at least the last few chapters of the book. In essence, in commercial fiction, story information is manipulated to build tension.

In literary fiction, information is used in different ways, and in writing the literary story, withholding information that would reasonably be known by the narrator—and characters—is not readily accepted and should be avoided. For example, in a literary story, a boarder might find his landlady stabbed to death by her piano student and we read to learn why and how. In genre fiction, the lady is found dead and we read to learn how the protagonist discovers and/or proves that the piano student was the murderer.

This judgment on withheld information is not often as black and white as indicated. The author must ask, in a literary story, will the reader feel manipulated by the withheld information in ways that a reader who enjoys genre fiction will accept and seek?

For the most part, readers of literary fiction want plot information presented when the story demands. This is the importance of evaluating information given and information withheld carefully so that it remains within what the reader will accept.

3. *Omniscience and point of view. How is information filtered?*

Since a story is a series of events (scenes) delivered through prose in a dramatic and meaningful way, the information delivered to the reader must be specific for the story and the desired effect of the story. Omniscience has different implications in different contexts, but it is important for a writer to define and explore what role omniscience plays in a story. In many contexts, omniscience may not be advisable for good storytelling, either in POV or the type of information provided to the reader.

For example, if a reader begins to assume a character is omniscient, then withheld information is manipulation to create tension. I'm telling the story, I know the murderer, and I'll tell you at the end. In character-based literary fiction, the character discovers information, and both the narrator and the reader know more or suspect more than the character. Characters who know more than the reader have taken over the story, closing the door on reader involvement.

For maximum value, in writing fiction, omniscience is best understood as an artificially created attitude about the way information is delivered. Omniscience as a noun means knowledge of all things real or apparent. Among writers, it is often used confusingly as an adjective—an omniscient point of view, for example. Omniscience is knowledge about all things; point of view refers to limitation of how things are described or told. Neither seems to complement the other. So when writers say "omniscient point of view" they could mean 1) a character or narrator that knows all about all things, or 2) multiple characters delivering a story through their established points of view. To further confuse the issue, some writers refer to omniscient third person or omniscient first person (usually referring to a character who is free to present information that he or she is not reasonably expected to know), or omniscient narrator, often in reference to story information delivered through many characters.

The use of omniscience as a presumed method of understanding how characters and narrators deliver information is not helpful for the writer who needs to be in control of a well structured, perfectly crafted story. The competent author needs control of how story worlds and real worlds vary, and how story information can be delivered.

Consider that in story writing we can define worlds differently for characters, narrators, and authors. The trick in writing is to deliver story information to the reader from the appropriate story world that is credible and maximally useful for drama and meaning, and this depends on how the reader interprets the source of information about the story. (This is true not only for clarity but also for credibility of the way the information is delivered, and for expectations of the veracity of the delivered information. Skillful authors seem to master these complexities to provide new levels of meaning and awareness in the reader.)

There are many worlds (again, world is a specified domain of human activity and the people involved): the author's world, which might be considered all-knowing within the thoughts and memories of the author's existence (and almost never used effectively in story telling by accomplished authors in modern fiction); the narrator's world, which might me considered all-knowing within the thoughts and memories of the narrator's existence; and a character's world for each character in the story, which is what each character thinks and remembers. Finally, there is the real world beyond human comprehension, God's world, where every truth about everything is known. Effective stories come from identifiable story worlds that are never omniscient, and always focused to present the best dramatic story possible.

4. Dos and don'ts.

> Avoid the term omniscience either as a noun or adjective when speaking of point of view.
> Evaluate all information delivered to a reader in the context of appropriateness for characterization and plot movement of the story.
> Use various points of view whenever it is clear that varying the point of view is the best way to provide critical story information at the desired point in the story.
> Do not allow unrelated information from non-story worlds of characters, authors, and narrators to creep into the storytelling.
> Keep in mind how far the point of view is from the action—the physical and psychological distance from the action—and choose the most effective points of view.
> Keep points of view credible, so the reader has no question whether or not the story information is credible, and there is a clear understanding between the narrator and the reader of the reliability of the point of view narration.
> Balance carefully appropriate craft techniques for delivery of story information: narrative summary, in-scene action, dialogue, and internal reflection.

➢ Avoid awkward points of view that result in unclear shifts in the story's presentation of time.

Chapter 9

Drama in Literary Fiction

1, *Drama: core thoughts.*

2. *Suspense.*

    Example 9A: suspense

    Example 9B: suspense with character-driven element

3. *Withheld information.*

4. *Drama is action.*

5. *Examples of description and showing.*

    Example 10A: Narrative description (telling):

    Example 10B: In-scene action (showing):

    Example 11A: Narrative telling

    Example 11B: In-scene showing.

Drama in Literary Fiction

1. *Drama: core thoughts.*

1. Great fiction is surprise, delight, and mastery.
2. Conflict-action-resolution is the writer's most essential tool.
3. Dramatic writing is more than just revealing prose.
4. Drama in literary fiction is mainly created through:
   a core story premise,
   unique and fully-realized characterization,
   and logical and acceptable motivation.
5. Drama in literary fiction is choosing well what information is best for the story and then providing that information predominantly in action scenes.

2. *Suspense.*

Suspense: feeling of uncertainty, excitement, or worry over how something will turn out.

Suspense contributes to drama, but it is not the sole element of drama in literary fiction. Suspense in literary fiction is the fear of something happening to a character we like or respect, and the character's personality affecting the outcome of plot elements.

Example 9A: suspense

Jane books a flight to New York to plead with her estranged husband. Her pilot arrives too intoxicated to fly the plane, successfully covering up his reduced capacities. Jane boards the plane. The pilot ignores the usual preflight checklist. The fuel tanks are less than a quarter full.

Readers experience a fear of something happening to a character, and if they like or respect the character, the suspense is heightened. Yet there is a lack in this plot construction of the character-driven element of literary fiction.

Example 9B: suspense with character-driven element

> Jane calls her clandestine lover to fly her to New York in his small plane to meet her estranged husband. She has made her lover distraught with her refusal to give up her efforts to patch her marriage. The lover arrives hungover from drowning his sorrows, and fails to complete a preflight checklist. The plane's fuel tanks have not been refueled.

This is not great writing but it does show how character-driven plots differ from circumstantial plots. Note how the second scenario also allows for complexities in the resolution that may reveal more about the characters and contribute to the meaning of the story—say, love is the root of disaster. The lover might sacrifice his life for Jane, or vice versa. Again, character generation of plot creates literary fiction. In popular fiction, the resolution may be simply a plane crash or an emergency landing and the arrest of the pilot.

3. *Withheld information.*

All stories have withheld information. As an author, you can only tell so much. The reasons why an author withholds information contribute to the quality of the story. When an author chooses to reveal story information is critical to story success; the expectations are different in genre fiction than in literary fiction.

Drama is conflict, action, and resolution. Characters are well developed with strong motivations and desires that drive the plot. The idea that withheld information will create suspense is rarely used in effective literary fiction. Withheld information may weaken the characterization and confuse the motivations.

In melodrama (using stereotypical characters, exaggerated descriptions of emotion, simplistic conflict and morality) crucial information is withheld to create suspense for a reader, but this is manipulation of the reader. The reader must accept this manipulation, too; the reader knows that the narrator knows who killed the rector but will accept not knowing until the end of the story to discover a fact. However, in literary fiction, all information crucial for the story (this is an author being true to the story and not using the story) is presented for the sole purpose of engaging the reader. Then the reader becomes involved in (and with) the characters resolving their conflicts—not in being told what is withheld—and the result is a change in the reader, a realization that nothing in their world will ever be the same because of their involvement in the story.

Let's say you write a story about a pregnant teenage girl, traveling alone cross-country for an abortion. For many authors, the story may be about the revelation of who fathered the child, and the discovery of this withheld information will delight many readers.

However, you could reveal all the circumstances of the pregnancy. What if it was incest and her father raped her, or what if the gym coach at school had seduced her during the trip to the finals in field hockey? Everything is up front. Now you set forth the structure to bring the reader into how the girl will solve her conflict—an unwanted pregnancy by someone she hates. You will reveal her nature and her capabilities. You will find a premise —forced lust destroys a normal life, for example. This way, you will engender understanding in the reader that enlightens or changes existing thought.

How story information is used in a dramatic context—whether delivered or withheld—is the skeleton of how different authors create their own unique stories. Authors of literary stories must not exploit a reader's interest and involvement through false handling of story facts. Instead, the reader must become involved in the story action and accept character change—and experience change in themselves.

4. *Drama is action.*

Most beginning writers do not have the instincts to write stories by creating conflict, action, and resolution in a series of scenes that present a story which will involve the reader. For the most part, beginners simply tell story happenings, often with complicated and inflated prose that is static and boring.

5. *Examples of description and showing.*

Example 10A: Narrative description (telling):

Paul was jealous that Helen could sing with so much passion that others couldn't take their eyes away from her as she performed.

Example 10B: In-scene action (showing):

Helen held the floor-stand microphone with both hands. The piano player played the introduction, hunched over the keyboard. Helen took a deep breath and sang with a soft, breathy voice, her eyes closed until the refrain, when her gaze swept the audience of strangers, all watching her.

She sang three verses and smiled at the end without a bow. The crowd applauded.

Paul approached Helen as she climbed down off the stage.

"I wish I could sing like that," Paul said. "I don't have your ear for perfection."

In-scene action and showing should be the major portion of a literary story, although narrative telling, when condensed—and not as a vehicle for asides, recall, and reflection—can be useful to advance the story efficiently.

Example 11A: Narrative telling. (Quick and effective, with time condensed.)

The ship sank.

Example 11B: In-scene showing. (More story time, more engaging, with time slowed and expanded.)

The ocean liner listed, taking on water through the hole the torpedo made in her portside. The bridge shuddered from two explosions in the engine room as the crew struggled to release the lifeboats, and the bow disappeared beneath the surface first, soon followed by the hull.

The feeling of momentum must not be lost in a story. The key is learning how to write with action (see also: Momentum).

Chapter 10

Desire and Motivation in Literary Fiction

1. *Definitions.*

2. *Principles.*

3. *Character Motivation.*

4. *How to use desire and motivation.*

Desire and Motivation in Literary Fiction

1. *Definitions.*

Desire: wanting to have something or wanting something to happen.

Motivation (or motive): the reason someone acts or behaves in a certain way.

Desire and motivation are essences of good storytelling, and are among the most defining features of literary fiction. In reality, desire and motivation are integral and dependent on all the other elements of fiction. The desires and motivations of characters may change, and certainly expand in ways that make them seem changed, with story development.

2. *Principles.*

As we look at what desires and motivations can do in a story, we should keep in mind these principles:

* In creating scenes, author knowledge of valid character desires allows writing that is maximally effective.
* For storytelling, core character desires that drive all action are more effective than superficial and poorly considered desires that are questioned, either consciously or subconsciously, by the reader as significant for motivation.
* Core desires of characters (and people) are not easily determined.
* Motivations interact and must be logical for story and character, and a change in a motivation expressed in scene, thought, or even back story will change the effects of other motivations.
* At times, identification and incorporation of desires and motivations in early story drafts is difficult, but as characters develop and action in the plot progresses, incorporation in later drafts and revisions becomes more practical, if not essential. Therefore, discovery of desire and motivations late in story creation often requires significant revision and restructuring.

Edict

In creating motivations, remember: significance (all consuming, with serious consequences), credibility (would this character, as developed, really do this?), emotion (action from specific feelings from the character, rather than abstract whimsy).

3. *Character Motivation.*

In essence, stories are about people, and to create great stories requires in-depth consideration of characters' desires and motivations. A character is not a few planks nailed together, floating down with the currents of a river to a calm sea; a character is, instead, a carefully crafted, one-person sailboat that must tack against the current, catching the right winds, struggling to move upstream to the river's gushing source. What makes the little sailboat struggle and why? It would be so easy to let the river dictate direction and destination. It is sad for modern literature that many contemporary stories are simply descriptions of real or imagined events of characters floating through life. Great fictional stories have logical desires and motivations that are embedded in the story's drama.

In memoir or biography, an author describes events that have happened and interprets what the perceived desires and motivations of the characters were from the actions in the story. In the fictional story, the author can imagine the best desires and motivations of a character, and these desires and motivations must be strong, must drive the plot, must be logical and credible with improvement by multiple revisions, and must heighten the impact of the character's reversal of thinking or enlightenment, i.e. theme and meaning. To be successful, the author must understand desires and motivations, build on desires and motivations with characterization, be open to the discovery of more effective desires and motivations as writing progresses, and be willing to revise in favor of the most significant desires and motivations. Finally, the desires and motivations must relate directly to character change in thinking or enlightenment that creates meaning in a story.

4. *How to use desire and motivation.*

As previously noted, the truth is plain: great characters are built layer by layer by actions and discovery, not just by describing features and traits, or by just describing feelings. Characters grow from every action made, every thought considered, and every word of dialogue spoken. Each molecule of character development must have some relationship to the matter it creates, and much of the cumulative, synergistic interaction of the elements of character development are created by the overriding effect of a strong desire, recognizable by the reader, and logical motivations as they relate to story and other character elements. Yet, paradoxically, most authors still describe characters from life, or imagined. It must be said again that describing characters, rather than creating them through action, removes the advantage of building a dynamic character who will act with desires and motives clear to the reader, propel the plot forward, and have some significant change in the thinking of reader and/or character.

It is also useful to rethink the process of revision. Revision is not the last chore to be completed after you get the work down on paper. Desires and motivations require much new thinking and discovery of new desires that better relate to key emotions. This often requires structural changes in the story—new beginnings, reshuffling of key scenes, etc.— that are better done before final draft stages.

Don't think of revision as prose adjustment. A story that fails to provide the desired effect cannot be corrected by intensifying and expanding the prose. In fact, failed stories are often over written because authors seek to convey significance through word choice, syntax, clever metaphors, and sentimentality when story structure and character desires and motivations need to be fixed. A significant story is created through actions woven into a beautiful fabric with the threads of desire and motivation.

Characters need unified, dominant, and strong desires and motives. This may not occur in life where we find people driven by many desires and motivations, often with random application to life's challenges. Characters are part of a structured story that requires significant and focused reasons for action. This allows for intensity in character development scene after scene and chapter after chapter, development that is cumulative and synergistic.

Core desires are fewer than might be expected and these core desires act as a premise underlying all character motivations in a story. Examples of good core desires for stories are not easy, but to get the idea, consider fear of eternal damnation as a better desire for an author to work with than guilt over a clandestine sexual experience. An unsatisfiable need for adoration provides broader application than an inability to pass by a mirror without looking at oneself. As character motivations are developed scene by scene, always seek the core desire that motivates. Then develop and revise accordingly, always seeking continuity from scene to scene.

Desire and motivation in literary fiction must be significant, but does not need to lead to violence or horror. Significant desire and motivation do not equate to murder, rape, or abuse of a child; significant motivations can result in beautiful interactions among characters. The literary fiction writer has the opportunity to create stories of lasting impact in dramatic and meaningful ways without always relying on violent or suspenseful action scenes. Literary fiction does not depend on the louder bang, the brighter flash, or the hotter fire for excellence. For the author, this is the joy and the challenge while engaging the reader through dynamic, dramatic writing.

Chapter 11

Momentum in Literary Fiction

Ideas to think about

1. Choose the right words.

      A. Verbs.

      B. Nouns.

      C. Adjectives.

      D. Adverbs.

      E. Concrete vs. abstract words.

2. Avoid obscurity.

3. Use proper constructions.

      Example 12: sentences.

4. Avoid poetics.

5. Make imagery dynamic

      Example 13: image.

      Example 14: image.

6. Adhere to in scene action.

      Example 15A: narrative statement—static, no action.

      Example 15B: same information developed in scene with action.

7. Avoid back story.

8. Make dialog active.

      Example 16A: failed dialogue.

      Example 16B: dialogue surprise and action.

Momentum in Literary Fiction

By tradition, literary fiction tends to be serious and static. A valuable area of improvement for literary writers is in making their writing vibrant with motion—full of energy that is transferred from page to reader. Action! All this action in writing comes from word choice, well-constructed sentences and paragraphs, and from clear transfer of ideas that avoids obscurity. Then a story has action in all its elements, and momentum overall.

Overall, everything should move forward in a story. A story is a tidal wave that carries water fowl, trees and plants, and man-made elements, broken and mangled; when it encounters obstacles it engulfs them and dislodges them inexorably. Stories cannot be stagnant puddles waiting for an occasional shower to maintain their existence. It is the author's challenge, if not duty, to create a tidal wave. It is a quest not accomplished in a few sittings before a computer screen. Learning to write with story momentum is a lifelong dedication, better learned by some than others.

Ideas to think about

1. *Choose the right words*

Words can have action or be inert, often with aspects of both. Authors, for the sake of the reader, need to use action words, but only when the word improves the meaning and effectiveness of the writing.

> **A. Verbs** (most important). Look for different degrees of action in the following examples. Note how action is related to specificity.
>
> ate—swallowed
> moved—walked
> understood—discovered
> told—described
> told—elaborated
> went—drove
> lay—reclined
> cooked—fried
> cooked—poached
> killed—bludgeoned to death
> began—ignited

NOTE: The use of certain verbs may convey a degree of action or a type of action that does not suit the scene or the narration. (Example: "His humor ignited her admiration" should not, in most circumstances, replace "She smiled at his joke." Authors need tasteful and accurate verb choices to develop pleasing writing styles.

B. **Nouns**. It is particularly useful in description of settings or any narrative in a story to choose nouns that have energy. When possible, image nouns should be concrete (hawk) rather than abstract (object). At times, no choice may be available, but when a choice is available, make it contribute to story imagery and momentum. Here are nouns that have different energies:

> rock–hawk
> telephone pole–computer
> road–river
> shadow–glitter

What story would you chose, a story about rocks, telephones poles and a road in shadow, or a story about hawks, computers, and a river that glitters? Right word associations can make good writing better.

C. Adjectives. Adjectives restrict a noun, or a verb form, and that can be desirable or undesirable. Compare adjectival forms and their effectiveness for lively writing.

Motionless steamroller. Waiting steamroller. Tilted steamroller. Rusted steamroller. Dead acrobat. Breathless acrobat. Plunging acrobat. Immortalized acrobat. Revered acrobat. Decaying acrobat. Perspiring acrobat.

Note: Adjectives are not equal in effect in a specific context; each has a different energy relationship to its noun. Authors must make the right adjective choices or their writing dies. Sometimes no adjective is best: "hear the crow" may be better than "hear the cawing crow," for example, because cawing is redundant—it is what a crow does if we hear it. On the other hand, certain adjectives are absolutely necessary for clarity. "White whale" means more than "whale" without an adjective. Authors improve by making better decisions about adjectives and other modifiers.

D. Adverbs.

Examples: talked – incessantly, or often, irritatingly, lovingly, uncontrollably, loudly, softly.

Note that every one of these adverbs could be replaced by a construction that showed rather than told. Example: for a "loudly" an author might use "when he shouted, little Jennie winced and covered her ears." However, this is probably too many words with too little of an effect. In this instance, maybe the adverb is better: "Jake spoke loudly to her."

In essence, adverbs can be valuable, brief sources of information. Still, authors must be in control of adverb choice and usage. Adverbs too often flag an author's unwillingness to seek out the right verb. She "yelled loudly" could be "screamed." "Moved rapidly" could be "jumped" or "ran" or "scurried."

Another disadvantage is that adverbs often confuse point of view (and narration) in storytelling. "He saw the enemy soldier unwillingly aim his rifle." The use of "unwillingly" briefly shifts the point of view to the soldier and outside the "He" subject of the sentence. Remove "unwillingly" and there is no point of view shift.

E. Concrete vs. abstract words. Concrete and abstract words have different effects on a reader. For action writing, concrete words are almost always better.

Examples: concrete and abstract words

concrete	*abstract*
tuberculosis	disease
Joe	population
Atlantic	ocean
March 22	future
tarragon	spice
violin	instrument
G note	sound
triplet	rhythm

As a writer, look for abstract words that need revision. Are there better, more concrete alternatives? Readers prefer a concrete word such as "violin" rather than "instrument" or even "musical instrument." Repeated abstractions cumulatively destroy good, creative writing while carefully chosen concrete words add pleasure to the reading and momentum of the story.

Words of caution: Fiddling with words alone cannot make writing great. Good writing has too many more important elements. Too often, writers spend revision time with words when structure needs change.

2. *Avoid obscurity.*

When a reader reads an author with muddled thinking, the reading slows, the reader's interest wanes, and the story is not successful. Action, so necessary in writing, is directly proportional to clear thinking.

Nothing will stagnate a story more than obscurity. Paradoxically, some authors believe obscure writing is clever and stimulating—but those are pseudo-intellectual ideas. In general, obscurity and vibrant writing do not mix in fiction prose.

A writer has an idea. It could be a concept or an image. The writer uses words and the arrangement of words to transmit an idea to a reader. It is not simple. Every human is different, with an individual way of thinking, unique past experiences, varied memory capacities, and degrees of learning. We assume that we think as most others and they assume the same of us, but there is wide variability. Authors need to learn to think clearly and logically to improve the understanding of their ideas by others, especially those who may not have the same thought processes. Above all, do not cling to mediocre ideas and obscure them in the belief that obscurity will make them seem better than they are.

Authors transmit clear thinking by accurate word association, careful attention to modifiers and antecedents, concrete rather than abstract ideas, and, for many, a mental image clarified before described. Authors must fine-tune their thinking so writing becomes effective in transferring ideas. The reward is not only good writing, but a sense of action for the reader.

3. *Use proper constructions.*

Authors write to be read; authors must avoid constructions or unclear associations that cause reading to be difficult.

A. Sentences. Choose the best sentence types for the prose of the story-moment.

Example 12: sentences

1) Periodic sentence (subject and verb at the end of a compound sentence). "With his body trembling and his breath trapped in his lungs as he failed to breathe, he jumped from the plane, pulling the ripcord."

2) Loose sentence (subject and verb at the beginning of a compound sentence). "He jumped from the plane, pulling the ripcord with his body trembling and his breath trapped in his lungs as he forgot to breathe."

The emphasis and effect is different. Both are valuable when used in an appropriate, receptive, creative-writing context. Sentence length and sound, as well as structure, should be also be varied with attention to rhythms and tensions of the story-moment.

B. Don't use a pronoun where the antecedent is not clear.

C. Don't present subordinate ideas when the relationship to the main idea is not clear.

D. Re-evaluate syntax: little changes can make significant differences.

The cat ate the mouse quickly.
Quickly, the cat ate the mouse.
The mouse was eaten quickly by the cat.
The hungry cat ate the mouse in a few bites.

NOTE: syntax must be adjusted throughout story creation for best effect.

4. *Avoid poetics.*

In general, avoid poetics. For example, do not use oxymorons. An oxymoron (figure of speech with contradictory terms: example—falsely true) can be an effective poetic technique, but is rarely, if ever, useful in fiction. Oxymoron, by definition, is unclear if not obscure. It is language in love with itself and in literary-fiction prose, it stops the action.

Alliteration (the same letter at the beginning of closely connected words: tiny tinsel-like tots teetering together) also stops a reader. Although useful in poetics when tastefully constructed, it is often amateurish in fiction.

Metaphor is the muscle that enlivens the skeleton of fiction and illuminates new understanding. However, clear metaphors are needed in fiction, and less so in poetry. In fiction, don't keep the reader guessing with obscure connections between the comparisons. Present clear metaphoric associations.

A simile, a type of metaphor, is an example. In fiction, it is essential that the comparison in a simile is perfect in logic (and accepted by the reader). A is like B in a way that makes the reader understand A better. A's comparison to B has to depend on differences between the two. If there is no difference, there is no effect. A rose is like a rose. No effect. The rose is not clarified for us. If there is too much difference and the comparison is unbelievable or not understandable, there is also no effect. Instead of saying "a rose is like a locomotive", try a closer comparison with a beauty connection. A rose is like a sunrise on the first day of spring. Not great, but a little closer to a successful simile.

(Note: A metaphor does not use like or as. A metaphor would be: "A rose is the first sunrise in spring.")

When writing fiction, make antecedents clear. Avoid constructions such as: "he would never use that to do this again." Even if the context provides some clues as to meaning, these vague pronouns frustrate a reader. Here is a possible improvement: "John would never use a spoon to dig a grave again." However, vague antecedents may be valuable for desired effects in poetry.

5. *Make imagery dynamic.*

As authors, we rarely think about momentum in imagery, but images in writing have useful characteristics to provide story momentum, unlike a photograph, which is a frozen instant, and static. It is strange that many authors write descriptive scenes as if recreating a photograph.

Movement in images is a privilege fiction gives to authors. In writing, images are created in a reader's mind, which is active in forming the image. Basically, authors don't create still lifes, they paint portraits that intrigue and engage the reader in scenes that live on the page.

Example 13: image

There was a bird on a limb.
Comment. Static.

The flying bird settled on the limb.
Comment. Improved with some action.

The olive branch quivered when the claws of the sparrow grasped the sturdy twig.
Comment. Lots of action. (Over done to emphasize the principle.)

Example 14: image

The locomotive with colorful cars behind it followed the track that snaked though the valley.
Comment. Any motion perceived is really implied.

Now with action:

The steam of the locomotive reddened the face of the engineer as he leaned out the window. The track curved many times ahead. He wondered, as the clouds gathered, if the printed banners with the Czar's name flapping above the red, green, and white decorations so carefully applied on the cars behind by the birthday celebrants, would be dampened, maybe even destroyed, by rain. He gripped the waist-high metal lever jutting up through a slit in the floor and shoved it forward. The locomotive strained ahead tilting to the left as it banked into the first turn.

6. *Adhere to in scene action.*

Example 15A: narrative statement—static, no action.

Janie adored animals. She went to the shelter and adopted a dog named Firefly that she loved at first site.

Example 15B: same information developed in scene with action.

Janie opened the steel door to the animal shelter on First Street. No one was behind the wooden table that served as a reception barrier. She walked back thorough a doorless opening into the converted two car garage. She stopped. Stacked cages lined each side of the passage. She held her breath at the foul smell. Barks and meows filled the air and she squeezed her eyes shut for a moment. She walked forward until she saw a white dog on its haunches, quiet except for a tail slowly moving back and forth, stirring up the sawdust at the cage bottom. The eyes looked directly at her, unfaltering. On the cage door was a tag that read "Firefly. 6/14."

In the back, the attendant was hosing down cages on a driveway.

"That dog, Firefly. I want to adopt him."

"Sorry, I think he's spoken for."

NOTE. In-scene action requires more reader time than narrative telling. Therefore, because it takes up precious storytelling time, in-scene action must have a legitimate purpose with significant reasons for inclusion to energize the story.

Ask these questions about use of in-scene action:

> *Does it develop the character?
> *Does it enhance motivation?
> *Does it contribute to physical movement through story time that is directly plot related?
> *Does it allow imagery and setting to be established subtly, without cumbersome self-importance?
> *Does it contribute to voice?
> *Is it related to theme and meaning?

If action doesn't do a lot, then a short narrative bridge may be best for the story.

7. Avoid back story.

Back story (anything that happened before the story begins), by its time relation to a story, affects and often stops the story's present momentum. What is the basic rule? Back story must advance front story. To check, always ask what a particular back story does for the front story. Answers might include: it provides needed characterization, is necessary for exposition, explains motivation, and others. In the good story, there is almost always a better and more effective way to provide for the reader than using back story.

8. *Make dialog active.*

Dialog needs to have action. This is accomplished primarily by word choice and ideation. It is also helpful not to have questions in dialog directly answered.

Example 16A: failed dialogue.

> "Is that a bear?" Joe asked.
> "Where?" Sam asked.
> "Over there."
> "Damn. I think it is a bear."
> "What are we going to do?"
> "I don't know."

Example 16B: dialogue with surprise and action.

> The bear reared back on its hind legs, roaring.
> "Don't move!" said Joe.
> "I'm going to throw up," Sam said.
> "He's seen us."
> "I dropped my rifle."
> "Start making noise. Maybe we can scare him."

Chapter 12

Parting thoughts: Part I

Parting thoughts: Part I

Literature needs to survive as a way of storytelling. For some stories, literature is the best presentation—usually with lasting meaning. Other stories do well with screenplay, stage play, memoir, or oral presentation. For literary writers and readers, the world needs great storytellers who think and write well and not great writers with no story telling skills.

The literary story is not the easiest writing, but it is the most rewarding accomplishment, bar none. The ideas in this text are for the writer who sees a story as art, and who wants to create a story that will remain in the collective memory of humans for future generations, like the works of Shakespeare, Chekhov, Tolstoy, Hemmingway, Faulkner, and Homer. Of course there is no suggestion in this presentation that incorporating the ideas will a make any author great, or that there are no other philosophies of writing that exist that may achieve greatness. There are many. However, the presentation does suggest that storytelling is essential for good fiction, and that the principles emphasized will help authors become better storytellers as a part of being good fiction writers.

Best wishes for every success in your writing career.

WHC

Literary Story as an Art Form:
A Text for Writers

Part II
Creating a Literary Story

Creating a Literary Story

Although any creative process written out will seem to be in steps, many of the creative actions will actually occur simultaneously. The most important skill to master is to establish early structure and characterization of a story as a unit (and not simply taking an idea and an image and writing to see what happens). Story success relates to revision before you write, then—with imagination—effectively crafting a story with conflict and action, motivation, and meaning. Every scene, and every bit of characterization, should be compatible with the imagined structure of the story and with the nature of the characters developed.

GOALS

STRUCTURE STORY
CREATE CHARACTER
USE DRAMA
REVISE WITH IMAGINATION
INCORPORATE THEME AND MEANING
ENGAGE THE READER AND ENTERTAIN

PROCESS OF CREATING A LITERARY STORY

Getting Ready

I. THE IDEA

    Discussion 1. SAMPLE STORY--IDEAS

II. TITLE

    Discussion 2. SAMPLE STORY--TITLE

III. CHARACTERS

    Discussion 3. SAMPLE STORY--CHARACTERS

    Discussion 4. SAMPLE STORY--EMOTIONS.

IV. STRUCTURE

    DISCUSSION 5. SAMPLE STORY--SCENE.

        A. Beginning

        B. Middle

        C. End

    Discussion 6. SAMPLE STORY--STRUCTURE

V. SCENE BY SCENE ANALYSIS OF SAMPLE STORY

Getting Ready

In your heart, to achieve as much as you can in writing, you must have a sincere desire to create a great story. You must not be consumed, or even be a little distracted, about how your writing will cause your reader to admire your prowess with words.

GREAT STORIES ENGAGE AND SUSTAIN THE INTEREST OF YOUR READER.

Many writers depend heavily on emotional prose based on abstraction and descriptive and reflective passages that are often static. Good stories require clear, but not necessarily fancy, prose that is scene-oriented, searches for drama that will be memorable, and has theme and meaning—not just a turn of events. When the writing succeeds, a story has well-motivated action that is credible for theme and character enlightenment.

Fiction writers have unique talents. They are imaginative and logical. Although fiction writers use the techniques of poets, who manipulate words and ideas, unlike poets, they structure stories with conflict and action in a series of interrelated scenes.

There is an indescribable satisfaction in creating a literary story as an art form. Not everyone is capable. What follows will give not only skills, but also ideas and attitudes that can make a difference and improve any writer's ability to tell interesting stories.

I. THE IDEA

An idea does not a story make.

It is common for people to see an interesting, unique character or to be moved by a certain event and believe it would make a fiction story. However, just because an idea is brilliant, or an event is profoundly moving, it does not necessarily make a story. Ideas are single frames in a feature length movie, a sentence in a Tolstoy novel, or a brush stroke on a painting. Stories are structured to make the story moving, memorable, and meaningful, while ideas are used to stimulate and materialize the writing. Even though ideas are essential as stimulus, to become a story an idea must be analyzed, expanded, placed in context, given characterization, fictionalized, and settled into the basket full of ideas that make up a story.

Nurturing an idea.

Ideas are essential to help stimulate writing, but they can never stand alone. Ideas must be nurtured. They must be shaped for the story as a series of interrelated events that present conflict, reaction to the conflict, and a resolution that has meaning.

An idea may not even be a starting point of writing the story. A significant idea frequently does not act as the first point in story development. Writers who have ideas and start to write without structure have bypassed an import aspect of storytelling—structure of a story for best drama. To be effective, authors need to engage the reader in character and plot, and not be associated directly with the idea that generated the story.

Reader emotions.

What emotion do you want the reader to feel? Awe? Sympathy? Terror? Writing to evoke a desired reader emotion makes the writing better, and ideas are the stem cells that grow into reader emotional fulfillment. However, if you create a story for a reader to experience an emotion and you fail, the reader will perceive the writing to be sentimental, demanding more feeling than is justified by the words on the page. For a writer to be successful requires a reasonable choice of reader emotion for the scene and story, and requires tempered writing.

Imagination.

Readers delight when they find imaginative writing, but writers despair at failure to activate imagination and use it effectively. Many writers believe imagination just is and is best if not thought about too much. However, writers can improve. Imagination can be found in the universe of alternatives for writers where fresh, unique, and vibrant thoughts are discovered that drive clear character thinking and action and assure reasonable plots.

Finding the conflict.

You see Niagara Falls in the light of a full moon and you love the power, magnitude, and mystery of the falls. As an author, you want to share the emotion with a reader and you decide a story is best. You have a brother-in-law who tried to kill himself with an overdose of prescription medicines. That is a traumatic event, but you see an opportunity to make a suicide work into the Niagara Falls story.

You write. A character is at the edge of the falls, ready to jump, to generate suspense and to allow description of the Falls. He's on the guardrail, facing the long drop, the frothing water, and the mist. People have been killed often during the past few years, and you give a flashback description example to capture the emotion. The character jumps and you describe his feelings of devastation as he jumps. You are satisfied you have expanded your idea into a story. Not really.

Stories are conflict and action that relate to a significant resolution, and simply telling emotions generated by ideas will not result in a valued literary story. Danger at the edge of the falls can create a modicum of suspense, but it is not engaging enough. Description of the Falls, no matter how glorious, will not evoke a significant emotional response in the reader. In the literary story, the reader is aware of the motivations of the character and the circumstances that will be precipitated by the action taken or not taken. With character driven action, the story becomes more alive and more engaging. There is no substitute.

How does a writer find conflict? If you just have the Niagara Falls character go into a men's room and swallow pills from a bottle full of aspirin and die, there is no conflict and no one will notice or care. Conflict is desire against opposing desire, desire against almost insurmountable obstacles, and desire against internal needs out of control—forces opposed. The opposition in conflict does not have to be good against evil, either. Often, good going against good, and evil against evil, are better.

There is a common belief that structure of ideas will squash the spontaneous lyrical magic of some writers, but structure and magic are not opposites competing for limited space. Both are inseparable elements of a good story. Where it seems that magical writing will only be found in chaotic, free-form thinking, magical writing is better supported by creativity shared and directed toward the structure of a story. Story and magical writing are the flesh and bones to a body; they are not competitive, nor are they as effective separately.

Readers appreciate great writing, but most readers love a story. Readers read to be involved rather than just informed. The author who works with the structure of conflict and action lets readers participate is creating the story they crave.

Ridiculous? Only if you haven't grasped the concept. This thinking is absolutely necessary for a literary story. It is what makes literary fiction special.

Ideas stimulate the process of story creation; they alone are not the process.

Discussion 1: SAMPLE STORY--IDEAS

The sample story was stimulated from two specific but unrelated events. These events were noted separately and joined as the story needed plausible and significant conflict.

The first idea was simply a humiliating memory from childhood. A little boy proudly created a ceramic ashtray in a school art class and it was destroyed by a jealous bully. He had no way to provide equivalent and satisfactory reactive pain and hurt on the destroyer. Although strong emotion was created in the author at the time, the idea didn't have enough easily molded significance for a short story or novel. The idea—boy's ashtray destroyed—isn't a lot to work with, but it did work out to be a precipitating emotion that led to other escalating conflicts.

The second idea was a memorable happening as an adult. An eight-year-old boy drowned in a river and the only witness was a companion about the same age. Nothing in the circumstance pointed to wrongdoing, but the child witness was, in the eyes of most people, capable of harming another. Fear in his mother's eyes showed her suspicions of the guilt of her son and she quickly proceeded to pronounce her son's goodness. Nothing ever happened. The boy became a doctor and the other child's death was never explained. The idea as related to a story was superficial and not well defined, yet there seemed to be value in exploring the suspicions of others on the suspect, especially if he were innocent. The idea came to contribute one theme to the story, the concept of injustice from false accusation, and the special qualities required of the one suspected not to become a victim of the circumstances.

As the story developed, this suspicion of guilt would fuel a self-righteous woman to enjoy her willingness to forgive—to guarantee her salvation. She mistakes this feeling of pride in forgiveness for love.

II. TITLE

It is rare that a good title comes easily. It is common to consider the title after all writing is complete, but that can be a failed opportunity. In fiction, titles can be an integrated part of the story, serving descriptive, enlightening, and even meaningful purposes. The title also attracts interest in, and attention to, the story, so time spent serves well.

Even of more value is incorporating the search for a title as a part of creating the story as a whole. Using the search for a right title can, like a yeast starter, precipitate thinking about theme and meaning, as well as character core desires.

In the beginning, any title will serve as a stimulus to consider story structure and will, as the story develops, be changed, upgraded, corrected, or discarded.

The search for a title early in the writing process can help with other creative decisions about the story.

Discussion 2: SAMPLE STORY--TITLE

"The Indelible Myth"

At the beginning, the working story title was "Bird and the Boy." It referred to a drawing the boy had made for his mother for Mother's Day that was destroyed, and it referred to the precipitating incident. But it was not the most important part of the story, so the title seemed superficial and needed to be changed.

In the final manuscript the title is "The Indelible Myth." "Justice" and "Injustice" were considered but were not specific enough. The idea of indelible seemed good, and the idea that the protagonist was innocent and all that was said was myth also seemed good. However, "The Indelible Myth" is not quite right. Someday the right idea will come and the title will be changed again. Still, thinking about a title while the story is written aids in thinking of the story as a unit.

Having a working title helps think about meaning and theme.

The right title for a story may not come until long after the final draft is completed.

III. CHARACTERS

From your idea(s), you must also imagine characters. Characters in literature are molded by their reactions to events with conflict and choices, or by a narrator describing the thoughts, feelings, and actions of a character. Both are needed but the former is most effective and should comprise the bulk of the story.

As the characters are molded in the story, the author is learning everything about each character, including traits that will never be placed on the page but that will contribute to the character development. To create better dramatic situations in the story, the author must know every character's desires. Core desires such as escape from something, demanding admiration, yearning for affection, jealousy that evokes action, revenge against a breach of honor, spiritual acceptance, and absolute power over someone (or others) are very important to a character,

Endings should be conceived and summarized in one or two sentences. The ending will affect character development. Endings will change or mature as the story develops, and this will affect the development of characters and should be addressed in revision. In fiction, a character cannot have a past that does not directly contribute to the ending. This is the lifeblood of story meaning, and honors a theme in a story.

As characters develop through action and thoughts in the story, each attribute becomes more important as the overall character is defined. Also, character desires and motivations must support the plot, theme, and meaning in a story.

Characters evolve rather than appear fully formed. The memorable character's evolution is dependent on a story's structure, meaning, and theme, and on the ending and the talent of the author.

Discussion 3A: SAMPLE STORY--CHARACTERS

Protagonist (unnamed 1ˢᵗ person). A pharmacist falsely suspected of murder as a child, a suspicion stoked by his need to take revenge after the unjust destruction of something he valued. He loved his parents and a special woman in his life. He was sensitive, artistic, but would fight when wronged. He is unreliable in the sense that the reader cannot know (for story effect) whether his evaluation of himself as an budding artist, his view of the town that is punishing him, or his prediction of children facing a horrid life, is an any way true or reasonable. However, he does not seem so unreliable that he would either deny it or would not tell the reader of his contribution to the child's death.

Miss Pritchett. Teacher. Admired by protagonist. Seems to have favorites that generate hostility. (Desire to be liked so much that she fails to see the advantage of objective honesty in dealing with her students. Note that even as a minor character, her desire motivates action in Ruth that promotes jealous violence.)

Leesville (town). The town's residents harbor suspicion that the protagonist was involved in some way with the mysterious death of a girl. The town is isolated, opinionated, proud, rigid, judgmental, and mean. A true antagonist, at least perceived.

Protagonist's mother. Loving and understanding. Always protective. Reasonable. In the 1ˢᵗ person point of view, this mother character is filtered, and there may be an element of unreliability; that is, the 1st person character gives a subjective reflection of the mother's true character. Yet this is not detrimental, even if the mother is not as presented it is the boy's view of her that is important to the story, and to change the point of view to third person for more objective truth about the mother would not make any significant difference in the story. It is enough to see the mother as her young son might see her.

Protagonist's father. Ineffective. Probably unfaithful, as he goes to Florida as soon as the mother dies with a woman he's known for years. He barbecues while the families search for a missing child.

Ruth. Insecure. Mean. Bully. Jealous. Probably suppressing an attraction to the protagonist.

Robyn Welter. Teacher, librarian. Desires children. Capable of love but restricted by her self-righteous need to forgive. She wants the protagonist to be guilty (unconsciously) so she can forgive and feel morally superior. A protestant Christian. Tendency to shirk life rather than live it (a librarian removed from vibrant life, a teacher of young children, directing rather than participating for change). Fails a crucial test in a moment of grace that causes her to lose the one she loves. A key character that must be painted in a few brief strokes to deliver impact in the story.

Characters not developed: sheriff, students, man on the street.

Discussion 3B: SAMPLE STORY--IMAGINATIVE ALTERNATIVES

In the sample story, the boy is innocent and unjustly suspected. However, what if the boy is suspected but never confronted and is guilty? The town's punishment is just—even inadequate. What if the boy grows up with constant rejection, constantly denying his guilt, and his anger grows to explosive levels so he is quick tempered and suspicious? He marries and becomes abusive. He is confronted by a minister who angers him to a point of violence. He is jailed for assault, but his wife continues to support him. Why does she love him? What motivates her? So the situation has changed, the story is new, and thinking about alternatives can improve an existing draft with new ideas or allow a stronger story to emerge.

Discussion 4: SAMPLE STORY--CHARACTER DESIRE AND MOTIVATION.

The emotions of characters in a story are complex, multiple, and strong but not easily identified, and they result in logical actions. To assure that there is credibility in the story, the emotions of all characters need to be held in as scenes are developed. Every action and every word said is generated and tempered by a character's feelings of the moment, and what those feelings are, their appropriateness for the moment, and their effect should be on the author's creative palette. The feelings should be addressed in revision for the appropriateness of their strength among the feelings of others for the moment, and for the logic of their progression as the story develops.

Protagonist. Pride and contentment. Anger at injustice. Despair over false suspicions. Love. Disappointment.

Fiancée (Robyn). Fear of rejection from insecurity, resulting in righteousness. Needs to love to have children. Despair at being rejected but unable to understand. Fearfully reticent to engage in human interaction.

Bully (Ruth) Angry at being a woman and wrongfully perceives herself as untalented at anything. Seeks out a younger child who is talented. Proud of her heritage, wealth, and status. Attracted to protagonist, in a love way. Embarrassed by her fantasies about the protagonist, blames him for her frustrations, and acts out.

Mother. Love for son, and a desire to have him succeed and be happy. Fear of injustice that makes her protective.

Minister. Disdain for the follies of others. Pride in fighting sin. But most important, a fear of being insignificant.

Protestant minister/therapist. Motivated by his belief that the entire world is populated by sin and that he is among the few that see the sin, confront it, and demand penance. He assumes the protagonist is guilty. He becomes a co-conspirator with Robyn in her need to intensify her self-righteousness. He is practicing therapy where he is neither qualified nor gifted. Arrogant. An evil man draped in religious cloth.

IV. STRUCTURE

Structuring a story

Literary stories are not a dinner table discussion of what happened today, or yesterday, or last year.

> "We went fishing yesterday. Sure enough. Mark and I hauled the boat down to the landing. We trolled for awhile in deep water, Mark falling asleep up in the bow. Laugh . . . thought I'd cry. Then we go to shallow water and Mark tries a few casts while I bring the boat in close to shore for him. The lure tangled in a low bush on the shore. He damn near fell in the water. I told him he'd better sit down or he'd be making smooch with those fish under the boat."

This is what an uncle might say at the dinner table, and it is the way that many stories are written. But core desires that create conflict are not evident. There is no drama that might build interest, much less eagerness to see what will happen. Why is this not a story? It is only a recounting, a telling of what happened. There is little controlled structure outlining scene with function. There is no attempt to develop the characters and there is almost no action.

How do you begin to insert the elements of story—conflict, action, and resolution? You use imagination. You do not limit your character development or plot in any way that is against a good story (in the mistaken belief that accurate descriptions of living make vibrant, meaningful stories). What if the "I" character in the dinner story doesn't want to go fishing? Mark is not a good sportsman and has hooked himself and others many times; he blinded his little brother's left eye when he hooked him with a cast last year. Mark stood up against advice and fell out of the boat once and almost drowned. He spent two days in hospital! The "I" wants to troll for safety, but Mark insists on casting near shore. His lure gets hung up in a tree. Against all caution, he leans closer to the tree. He pulls the boat closer to shore. A water moccasin drops from a limb into the boat. Mark panics. The "I" tells him to calm down and begins to hit the snake with an oar. Mark picks up a loaded shotgun and shoots. He wounds the "I" and sinks the boat, and the snake swims off.

Of course this is not what anyone would write for a literary story, but you can see how conflict, action, and resolution might be injected into a story.

Authors structure stories to achieve maximum enjoyment for the reader using skills of both storytelling and writing. In essence, readers want to experience an emotional response and enlightenment from a story. Of course they will enjoy other types of writing, but the literary story is special.

Structuring a story addresses essential story elements. 1) Structure directs the action of one or more main characters. 2) Structure aids in character development. For example, characters need hero qualities and structure helps to identify opportunities. This is also true of courage, an essential trait that readers want to identify with. 3) Structure helps assure that early motivations are logical when they precipitate action later in the story. 4) Structure defines scenes and characters so they are focused on the essential emotional and plot progress of the story and the resolution of conflict.

As the author reviews the structure of the story, there must be something that the character must acquire or achieve, and it must be clear that all structural elements support awareness of this need. This need cannot be abstract and should be identifiable, clarified, and incorporated as part of structure. Example: A desire for love, revenge, and attention must be translated into specific and easily identified goals at the scene level: Jane to marry me; an eye for an eye to the murderer of my beloved wife; the widest recognition for my talent as the writer of my novel, *Kneecaps*.

Many writers will believe in and think of admired examples of stories that are unstructured and simply told, letting conflicts emerge when the story seems to present them. In fact, many stories are published that were proudly created without structure of conflict and action. Such writers should consider two important ideas. First, the conflicts and action created in the examples do not represent the skill of presentation of the writers of great stories. Significant and effective conflicts are often subtle and submerged in a story. Second, stories void of action and conflict simply do not reach their potential for a reader's emotional involvement, enlightenment, and enjoyment.

Discussion 5: SAMPLE STORY--SCENES

Progression/action outline

Scene 1. Setting. Town of Leesville.
Scene 2. School room. Establish pride in drawing. Admiration from others (some reluctant). Love of mother and desire to make her happy. Establishment of time of being young (forth grade).
Scene 3. Hours later. Corner. On way home. Attacked by an older girl who destroys his drawing; He attacks. He is seen as the aggressor by the adults who break up the fight.

Scene 4. Months. Transition from attack to picnic. Imposed punishment by school and town.

Scene 5. Picnic at Ruth's house near the river. Disappearance. Search. Death.

Scene 6. Transition. From death to moving away. Suspicion, rejection. Isolation.

Scene 7. Confrontation with fiancée and minister. Fiancée failed moment of grace. Rejection of fiancée. Determination to go on.

Beginning, Middle. and End

Although you may never need to graph your story in blocks, it is useful to have a general idea of the relative size of sections of a story. Beginnings are orienting the reader to characters and conflict, setting and theme; the middle is the conflict and the action (where most of the development takes place); and the ending is conflict resolution with meaning.

Discussion 6: SAMPLE STORY--RELATIVE SECTION SIZE

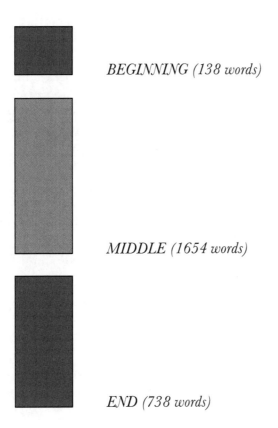

BEGINNING (138 words)

MIDDLE (1654 words)

END (738 words)

Use of structural blocks for beginning, middle, and end for the sample story allows clarified thinking about story structure. The sample story middle covers many years and is told primarily in narrative. It incorporates the conflict of the myth and reality. The end covers only a few minutes of story time and is focused on conflict with the protagonist and his fiancée, and is primarily in-scene. Overall, the events are chronological and related, but there are at least two ways to consider the structure of the story. First, is the story essentially a scene in a minister's office with the protagonist's life summarized as back story before the scene is presented? This lends itself more to a point of view restricted to the 1st person. Or, is the story told chronologically? This thinking lends more to a more prominent narrator presence (even in 1st person) with the tone and emotional valence possible with the narrator voice. This view also tends to suggest a telling more distant from the happening of the story.

Of course, much of this develops instinctively with good authors, yet learning to use structure can add a dimension of excellence to the author's talents and skills.

In the sample story, structural considerations may be restricted but amplified in need by the short length of the story, a condition set for the story to be used as an example.

A. Beginning

The engagement of the reader by the character(s), an essential part of telling a literary story, must come early. Below are essentials in engaging the reader in a character. This engagement must headline the story through structure so the reader is not distracted, and so the scene-by-scene story development works.

Essentials of early reader engagement with character(s)

1. *Hero* (traits that we would like to have and experience). In some way, the character must be larger than life, usually just a little, to maintain credibility in literary fiction, but still significant enough to maximize reader satisfaction. Readers will identify with genre super-heroes like Superman or the Terminator because they want to experience extraordinary physical and mental capabilities. In general, in literary fiction, hero qualities need characteristics of being able to exist in the reader's world, and allow a memorable and lasting emotional sympathy with the character. With super-heroes, an expansive suspension-of-disbelief is required for the story, and what

happens to the character does not achieve the significant human-like impact so important to literary fiction.

2. *Suffer unjustly*.   All humans identify with someone unjustly accused, punished, humiliated, or under-appreciated.

3. *Humor*. Humans love to laugh. A humorous character is easily accepted even when unlikable or not admired. An ironic character is also useful.

4. *Belief in action*. Readers should support the character's motivations for action; that is, agree or at least understand motivations for action.

5. *Imminent danger*. Humans sympathize with characters in danger from internal or external sources.

6. *Courage*. Readers identify with courage (ability to face danger, obstacles, pain, or the unknown without paralyzing fear or deflection from purpose). In literary fiction this can be courage to face seemingly restricted emotional obstacles, even the slightest of unjust inequities, and does not need to simply be courage in the face of physical danger like battles or end-of-the-world scenarios.

7. *A strong character desire or need*. Readers accept desires that they can understand and sympathize with.

8. *Cleverness*. Readers attach to intelligent, clever people. At times, a character as trickster, especially if young, can engage a reader.

B. Middle

A story is a series of interrelated scenes, and the middle is where these scenes develop. It is here where characters face their conflicts and act in believable and meaningful ways. In the middle, the story should never wander from the theme or the progression to the ending. For example, action should not be created just for characterization alone without contribution to plot progression, and vice versa.

Action and conflict.

A protagonist can be in conflict with nature, or with himself or herself. However, human conflict is most often person against person. It allows more effective action in scenes, and it allows credibility and intensity of conflict.

Authors must avoid action without conflict. For example, in a story, a protagonist might want to obtain the new and unmarketed vaccine for his lover who is at risk for AIDS. There is no legal way to acquire the vaccine and he decides to bribe a healthcare worker to help him steal the vaccine from a research laboratory. In the story, the lover can't pop up and say, "No need, I found it on the Internet and it came in the mail from Canada yesterday. All is well." No conflict results in unproductive action—and no story.

Focused goal.

The reader will be more involved if the goal of an action scene is more concrete than abstract, and this is more important for shorter fiction where development is, of necessity, limited. In general, an abstract goal such as happiness or the need to be loved cannot be developed effectively as a character's specific goal—for example, robbing a bank to go on vacation to be happy or screwing my friend's sister to find love.

C. End

In structuring a story and in defining scenes and characters, the author must have an ending in mind that is directly related to the theme and meaning of the story. The major character's desire is essential, and should be, through structure, within the definition of every scene. Similarly, the resolution of the conflict that comes at the end is the result of the action of every scene, and must relate to theme and all characters' desires in reasonable ways.

Discussion 7: SAMPLE STORY--STRUCTURE

Beginning. Because the story is short, the beginning is used only for scene, time, and attitude of the town that will later affect the protagonist. Some aspects of the protagonist's character are revealed.

Middle. The middle provides the reader with something to care about in the protagonist. The protagonist in the sample story is artistic, loving, and has a sense of justice. He is respectable. He retaliates violently against a larger, older student—albeit a girl—to justly defend the destruction of something dear to him that he was to give his mother. Most readers would sympathize.

The middle section has a number of scenes that develop the conflict —suspicion and rejection. The girl's accidental death and the town's suspicion that the hero might be involved put his reputation and his confidence in himself in jeopardy. He must leave and go elsewhere to grow and shed this undeserved reputation. He is moral, and he has a certain courage to refuse to be victimized. Most readers would sympathize. All of the middle section prepares for the end.

End. In one of the most important conflicts of protagonist's life, he tests his fiancée's belief in him by revealing the details of his background, and she fails to love him unconditionally. Instead, she has pride in her self-righteous forgiveness of his action. She pities him, and reveals her belief that he might be guilty. In essence, she had a moment of grace and fails because of her own weakness—her self-righteousness.

Philosophy of Structure

Structuring the story before you write a scene is essential for improvement in story writing. Admittedly, this part of the process is often ignored for literary writers. In fact, the modern writer often starts a character on a story journey, writing each scene as the character progress, imagining within the limitation of the scene. This decreases the effectiveness of the writing. Every writer needs to know where the story is going and what happens in the ending and, through structure, make the story a unit that serves the single purpose of carrying the reader through an enjoyable interlude in their lives.

Structure keeps story ideas from being pearls on a string. Structure identifies ideas that permeate into a story and keep the story focused and interesting, as yeast in dough has an internal but overall effect that allows a tasty loaf of bread to rise.

SUMMARY: WHY STRUCTURE A STORY?

TIMELINE. Readers need an overall orientation to the time of the story and how time is presented as the story progresses. Authors who utilize structure write with clear timelines embedded in story.

NARRATIVE VOICE. Consistency of voice is essential for great stories. Voice may change, with positive effect, as a story progresses, and structuring keeps narrative voice reasonable as changes occur.

POINT OF VIEW. Structure allows maximum effect in choice of point of view. Some story information is best presented by a specific point of view. Structure allows accurate identification of the best point of view.

CHARACTERIZATION. Structuring assures continuous characterization throughout the story and allows readers to identify with the plot where characterization can be maximally developed.

PLOT: PACING. No reader wants to be rushed through a story or, at the other extreme, wants to stagnate from lack of story movement. Structure provides a monitor for pacing of story action and character change.

THEME AND MEANING. Structure helps prioritize scenes and characterization that support the theme and meaning of the story. As important, structure helps identify extraneous material for removal.

EMOTIONS. One of the most difficult tasks for an author is to provide emotional impact in the right context and at the right time to make the story live. Structure is almost essential to identify and best use characters' emotions for the most impact in a story, particularly the logical actions emotions precipitate.

MOMENTUM. Structure, because of its eagle-eye viewing of story action, is best to identify static scenes and failed energy for writing.

V. SCENE BY SCENE ANALYSIS OF SAMPLE STORY

SAMPLE STORY SCENE 1

Leesville clung to the banks of the Percumsah River, as did Natchez, on a much grander scale, on the Mississippi River on the opposite side of the state. Citizens of Leesville were born and raised within twenty-five miles of the town's center and it was rare for a family to leave for the outside world; no people from afar that I remember ever permanently settled in Leesville when I was growing up. Although a few tried, they always moved on.

Leesville's residents had their own way of thinking in the 1960s. They didn't celebrate Lincoln's birthday, even though it was a national holiday, but they closed the schools to mourn the death of Jefferson Davis. Above my school, a confederate battle flag was raised at sunrise and lowered at sunset, without the stars and stripes. It wasn't protest, just habit.

ANALYSIS SCENE 1

Place: Northern Mississippi.

Time: 1960s. Information is provided from a time later than the story's time, but not close to the reader's time in the real world.

Technique: narrator and/or 1st person. When 1st person, probably well after the time of the story ending. This is an example of narrator function in a 1st person story. (The information about the population not changing is from a narrator's view, even though mixed with 1st person POV. This is important only to demonstrate how a reader might interpret a narrator's presence with more reliability and objectivity. A narrator knows more about the story, and the narrator is less likely to be swayed by the emotions and opinions of the 1st person. This is often an important function in 1st person—and all points of view.) An effective author should recognize a distinct narrator voice, even in first person, and choose the most effective voice and POV.

Action: Leesville described as setting. Purpose: to create a small, isolated Southern town that is capable of unfounded, wrong, headstrong opinions. Town to act as a character in conflict with protagonist.

Alternatives: This section could have been placed firmly in the first person point of view, but this leads to awkward exposition in the writing. For example:

> I was walking to Leesville Elementary School, where I was in the fourth grade. A confederate battle flag flapped in the breeze on a pole jutting above the roof line. I never saw the Stars and Stripes there.
>
> Leesville was on the river. It wasn't navigable, but it flowed steady enough to be hard to swim in. The only bridge across the river was about a mile north of town, and the people stayed pretty much to themselves. Few strangers moved in and few natives left.

The exposition about strangers and natives and the description of the bridge out of scene (to establish town isolation) is an awkward insertion of information as the protagonist is walking to school. It would be an action stopper to include that information.

This exposition and back story through 1st person narration seems forced and it affects the quality of the writing. The issue should be perceived as information needed by the reader and information that should be presented so the reader is not distracted from the story. The original scene written has a narrator presence; the narrator here is distinctly different than the narrator who speaks often throughout the story. Both are the same first person, but their time of speaking is at different stages in the life of the narrator, and the older is more objective than the younger.

SAMPLE STORY SCENE 2

> When I was in the fourth grade, my art training was with Miss Patchett in a Thursday afternoon session with students from many different grades. In May, we were creating Mother's Day gifts; I drew a bird. It took a full two hours, and Miss Patchett stopped by often to see my progress. Then, before the bell rang, she singled out my bird as the best accomplishment of the day. She held it in front of her, the top edge gently squeezed by thumb and index finger, and rotated from side to side for all to see. Most of the kids my age frowned and wished their art had been chosen. The older kids closer to high school smiled

at what they thought was a lack of sophistication. But it was special, everyone knew it in their hearts—a narrow snipe-like bill, long legs and three toed feet, a perfect circle for a head with a yellow eye, alert yet kind. The thrush-size body had reds and yellows and tilted forward, the tail fanning out behind, the wings with the greens and deep blues of a peacock.

ANALYSIS SCENE 2

Place: grade school in Leesville.

Time: The beginning of story will progress chronologically over many years in a short space of reader and story time. Long stories with short reading time require special attention to transitions.

Technique: 1ˢᵗ person. Narrative telling of action that occurs over an afternoon. Readers observe a scene, but do not engage in the scene. The 1ˢᵗ person POV is in forth grade. Later it is clear the 1ˢᵗ person narrator is an adult in his thirties.

Action: The boy draws a beautiful picture to give to his mother and is praised in front of the class by the teacher. Children are jealous. He is proud.

SAMPLE STORY SCENE 3

After school I headed home alone. My mood was buoyant. School was exciting and my parents loved me. I was really their only child. My sister, my only sibling, died at birth at the hospital and I never saw her.

I walked steadily, eager to see my mother. I had my book bag strapped to my back and carried my drawing in one hand so there was no chance of smudging the surface. I held it facing out and tried to be casual but I wanted the world to see what Miss Patchett had been so proud to display to her students, and what I was going to give my mother.

As I neared the corner to my home street off Elm, I saw Ruth, a girl who was a grade above and lived near the river. Usually her brother walked her home, and except for a few taunts, they usually ignored me. Her father was a doctor.

Today Ruth sat alone with her back against an oak tree, her books at her side. She was looking down at something in her hand. She was big for a girl, with strong, muscular legs and thick upper arms. She had short, dark brown hair and a wide, thick-lipped mouth with spaces between the teeth in front — not ugly really, but they held your attention. I circled around so as not to be close.

"That's a stupid bird," she called to me without looking at me.

I began to cross to the other side of the street, away from her. She stood up. She was in my art class. She must have remembered what Miss Patchett said about my bird.

"A really stupid, stupid bird." She stood, leaving her books, and came toward me. I moved quickly but she was too fast and she snatched my drawing and backed off. She had torn the bird into small pieces by the time I reached her.

My rage empowered me. With my fists I pummeled her, I pushed her down. I did not kick her, but I hit her again and again with my book bag, the brass buckles cutting her face and neck. Blood oozed from her forehead; she cried out and I hit her in the mouth with my fist, felt the pain as her teeth broke skin on my knuckles.

Two adults came. They held me away from her. I tried to explain about the bird, but they saw me as unreasonable and out of control. I quieted and waited until Ruth's parents were found to take her to the hospital, and my mother came to get me.

ANALYSIS SCENE 3

Place: on a street on the way home from school.

Time: immediately following previous scene.

Technique: The first and last parts of the scene are told in narrative with dramatic elements in the middle, plus a brief in-scene action segment. There is exposition (about family). There is a trace of humor (Ruth description). Note that the humorous tone and idea about Ruth again establishes the distance of the story teller from the time of story action. If the need is to be engaged in the action, the 1st person is too young and too involved in his apprehension about Ruth to be making ironic observations about her teeth.

Action: boy walks home. Ruth destroys his drawing and he retaliates by hitting her and pushing her down until he is restrained by adults.

SAMPLE STORY SCENE 4

Through tears I told mother about my bird, and she held me. I told her about my rage at Ruth destroying my gift without reason. And Mother said she loved me. But Ruth's parents demanded I be punished. The school was contacted to impose penalties; Ruth's parents thought I should be sent to reform school in New York. I was placed on probation and required to attend counseling sessions with my mother with the local pediatrician who had majored in psychology in college. The pediatrician was intent on reconciliation, and in time included Ruth's mother in some of the sessions with him and my mother. My mother and Ruth's mother came to an understanding and, I believe, liked each other in addition to gaining a mutual, if not at first hesitant, respect.

ANALYSIS SCENE 4

Place: a transition, not anchored in any place in particular but still in Leesville.

Time: many weeks.

Technique: narrative telling.

Action: boy tells his mother of his trouble and is comforted. Description of consequences and punishment. Mothers of the two children become wary friends at the suggestion of the counselor.

SAMPLE STORY SCENE 5

I survived my probation and my counseling. My family began to share family gatherings with Ruth and her parents, and her brother, who was much older than I. It was a Saturday, and Ruth's parents had invited our family over for an afternoon barbecue. Ole Miss was playing LSU away and a radio had been propped on a windowsill of the house with the volume on maximum. The adults sat in folding lawn chairs around a brick lined barbecue pit with a pig on a spit that Ruth's father, the doctor, basted sauce on every few minutes. Ruth's brother went to shoot squirrels with a twenty-two near the dump, refusing to take Ruth and me. Ruth decided to fish on the river, a skill her brother had taught her, usually on the oxbow about a mile north. Ruth's mother insisted I tag along. Carrying her rod and tackle box, Ruth went to where the river narrowed, the surface white with froth swirling in eddies. I followed. There was a floating dock with a planked walkway that tilted up slightly now that the river was high from recent rains. The river grumbled and swished here. She stood at the dock's edge in her bare feet and cast a lure awkwardly upstream.

"Are there fish here?" I asked.

"There are millions of fish," Ruth said.

"Like brim?" I asked.

"All kinds. Like every kind in the whole world."

After that, she did not speak to me. I soon walked away back to the house. I threw a tennis ball for Ruth's father's black lab to retrieve. When it was time to eat, I was sent to tell Ruth. But there was no one on the dock. I returned to tell the adults.

"Where is she?" Ruth's mother said.

I didn't answer.

"Have you done something to her?"

"I'm sure she'll be here soon," my mother said, coming and standing close to me.

"You're an evil child," Ruth's mother said to me.

"That's not fair, Martha," my mother said. "He's done nothing."

But Ruth's mother, breathing fast through clenched teeth, was already sending people out in different directions to find Ruth.

"I'm sure everything is all right," my mother said, taking me with her as she followed Ruth's parents to the river. My father tended the grill.

An hour later, Ruth's body was lifted from the water a few hundred yards downstream. I stood back at the edge of the crowd, but I could see her face was scratched and her leg bruised. Her fishing rod was never found.

ANALYSIS SCENE 5

Place: Ruth's house in the yard and at the river near the house.

Time: an afternoon.

Technique: in-scene action and some narration.

Action: families cooking out. Ruth goes fishing. Protagonist goes with her but leaves to throw a ball for the lab to retrieve. Ruth missing at dinner time. Families search. Ruth found dead.

SAMPLE STORY SCENE 6

The sheriff questioned me on the day Ruth died. Then later, twice, once for three hours, I sat at the police station as we went over every second of that afternoon. But nothing happened and I went back to school in the fall. I thought life was as it should be, except that Ruth's parents never spoke to me and walked away when they saw me, even at school.

But life was not as I expected. Little things happened, which now seem unimportant, but that were etched into me. Adults looked over me when they talked where children were allowed, and teachers rarely called on me in class. In gym I was passed over when the teams were chosen, and even at Church in the children's choir when I usually sang my lead in "Down by the Riverside," from the front row next to the sopranos, I was told to stay in the back next to tone-deaf Arthur whom no one liked. Later that year "Just a Closer Walk with Thee" replaced "Down by the Riverside" and I had no solos.

My mother became my only confidant. I told her how I was treated. I told her I didn't care what people thought, but I did care and couldn't sleep well. I was haunted by formless nightmares with sensations of falling, prolonged and slow to wake me. On weekends, I often went alone to sit motionless and silently by the river, near where Ruth died. Mother had conferences with my teachers and the principal, who seemed sympathetic and said I was a good boy and a hard worker. They trusted me, they said. They definitely thought Ruth's mother's tirades against me about her daughter's death would stop, and soon be forgotten.

I graduated from high school in the top half of my class, but at the ceremony, when the principal handed me my diploma and shook my hand, his eyes never tried to see me as he did with others, looking instead beyond me to someone in the audience. My mother died when I was away at my third year in a Birmingham college and my father retired and moved to Florida with a woman he'd known since high school.

I did well enough in college to win a scholarship to pharmacy school. I've been in practice now for four years and I am the manager of a drug store in Dayton, Ohio. I never speak of my past and I can't remember when, or if, anyone asked.

ANALYSIS SCENE 6

Place: unspecified.

Technique: narrative. Narrator tells of transitions that cover years. The narrator is the protagonist telling story from a later time and there is distance from story action in this section.

Time: next day to beginning of final scene (years of story time).

Action: Protagonists progression through story with accomplishments and losses.

SAMPLE STORY SCENE 7

But I must tell my story now. I have a decision to make. A woman (Robyn Welter) loves me. She is a small, frail woman of thirty-five, two years older than I, quiet, gentle, and shy. She is a school librarian, and teaches English to fourth graders. I love her too, and we want to marry. A date has been set. But as the time has come closer, I cannot find it in me to want children. Robyn wants a family. It is what will fulfill her life. It has become a source of contention and many tears, and I have come to wonder if marriage is right for me. I do not want children. I do not want to see them grow up.

We have come to the church office of her minister here in Ohio, for consultation. She is religious, and I believe in God but have little faith in the church. Robyn and I sit in chairs in front of the minister's desk. He is a young, unmarried man with glasses and a nervous glance that lands on others at odd times, disjointed in some way, avoiding contact as if he couldn't face the realties he might see by looking into another's eyes. Robyn and the minister discuss our incompatibilities and after an awkward silence, I just tell my story without emotion. It is a slice of potential reality that I do not want to force on a child I foster. When I finish, Robyn expresses her love for me again, and looks immediately toward the minister who smiles and nods.

The minister mumbles something about perceptions and justice. Then his voice strengthens.

"I must be honest," he says not looking at me, "You need to address this guilt. It seems to have consumed you. For a successful marriage, you must confront your inner demons."

I stare at him, not sure exactly of his meaning. I say nothing. I am not demonic.

He continues. "Your guilt frankly seems excessive for what you describe. Is there something that day by the river you might have repressed? Some nudge? Some hesitation to save her?"

I look to Robyn. It is, for her, the moment when she can make our marriage whole by believing in me. A marriage with children, too. In her soul, she must know that even as a child I was incapable of murder, or even assisting in an accident. That is what she must communicate to me.

She stares at me. At this instant I look into her eyes, tenuous in their lock on me, then she looks to her left, toward a table with a framed photo of a modern painting of Jesus in a romantic pose, holding a shepherd's crook. I continue to stare at Robyn, despair sweeping over me. She looks back. Now her eyes do not hold the sparkle and desire of our lovemaking. They hold pity. I slowly rise, button the front of my white lab coat, bow slightly to both if them.

"Don't run," the minister says.

"Please," Robyn says.

"Hypnosis," he says. "To explore your unconscious."

"You were a child," Robyn adds.

Who did nothing wrong, I want to tell her. But the well of doubt, once discovered, can never be erased.

"We could discover the facts," the minister says.

But we know the facts.

I exit to the street. I am surprised at how calm I am, still unaware of the weight of my resolution. I refuse to believe there is an evil memory inside me that will satisfy the omnipresent suspicions. I will bury myself in the demands of my profession. Alone, I will make my contributions to the world.

I pace away from the church until I am sweating, even though dark clouds swirl above and the chill of winter is already on us. I sit down on the low wall near the Air Force base. The street traffic is heavy. A near freezing rain begins to fall and the windshield wipers on cars that stop for the streetlight slap from side to side. I tremble, then sag, my arms are limp. "Bitch," I say. The minister is a fool. It is only Robyn, whom I love, who could pierce me with my own doubt about what I remember and what happened that day.

"I am without sin," I say aloud to a passing stranger who looks at me oddly without breaking stride.

ANALYSIS SCENE 7

Place: minister's office in church. Dayton, Ohio.

Time: story "present." Protagonist in thirties. About mid 1970s. All suggested, rather than described.

Technique: in-scene action. Switch to present tense. This tense change is problematic in that, to many, it might seem artificial and erode the credibility of the story. It seems useful, however, because the reader is close to the action and the narrator "I" is speaking during the time of the story's action. This should increase the impact of the conflict on the reader.

Action: The protagonist has told a story (which has been presented to readers in middle segment). His fiancée wants children. His unhappy childhood makes him hesitant, but not unwilling. He waits for his fiancée to support his innocence. Instead she forgives him. He sees that her love is based on forgiveness of his presumed guilt rather than on the belief that he could never do anything to take a person's life. He realizes, despite his love for her, that he cannot marry.

MEANING AND THEME IN SAMPLE STORY

To just be a literary story, the story must convey an awakening to some thinking previously thought or an enlightenment to new thoughts. Theme and meaning may not need to be defined by a reader. Not infrequently an emotional response is often precipitated by thoughts, and the result is enjoyed without the need to define theme and meaning. Yet, theme and meaning are still there, skillfully created by the writer.

In the sample story, the "I" protagonist comes to realize he will never be free of unjust suspicion and can never do anything to erase it or achieve justice. There is also meaning in the failure of the fiancée to believe. Instead she forgives, and it is a reaction the condemns the one she loves as well as herself.

The inability of "religion" that believes that sin rules the world, and religious salvation comes only by ferreting out the wicked and condemning them, can be unfair to the innocent also is part of the theme.

A major positive character trait is the refusal of the "I" to become a victim. He faces life, discouraged but without rancor, with what he has been given, and he does not allow his circumstances to overwhelm him.

These ideas, if valid for a reader, may result in an emotional and intellectual awareness that may make the story valuable.

SAMPLE STORY WITHOUT INTERRUPTIONS

The Indelible Myth

Leesville clung to the banks of the Percumsah River, as did Natchez, on a much grander scale, on the Mississippi River on the opposite side of the state. Citizens of Leesville were born and raised within twenty-five miles of the town's center and it was rare for a family to leave for the outside world; no people from afar that I remember ever permanently settled in Leesville when I was growing up. Although a few tried, they always moved on.

Leesville's residents had their own way of thinking in the 1960s. They didn't celebrate Lincoln's birthday, even though it was a national holiday, but they closed the schools to mourn the death of Jefferson Davis. Above my school a confederate battle flag was raised at sunrise and lowered at sunset, without the stars and stripes. It wasn't protest, just habit.

When I was in the fourth grade, my art training was with Miss Patchett in a Thursday afternoon session with students from many different grades. In May, we were creating Mother's Day gifts; I drew a bird. It took a full two hours, and Miss Patchett stopped by often to see my progress. Then, before the bell rang, she singled out my bird as the best accomplishment of the day. She held it in front of her, the top edge gently squeezed by thumb and index finger, and rotated from side to side for all to see. Most of the kids my age frowned and wished their art had been chosen. The older kids closer to high school smiled at what they thought was a lack of sophistication. But it was special, everyone knew it in their hearts—a narrow snipe-like bill, long legs and three toed feet, a perfect circle for a head with a yellow eye, alert yet kind. The thrush-size body had reds and yellows and tilted forward, the tail fanning out behind, the wings with the greens and deep blues of a peacock.

After school I headed home alone. My mood was buoyant. School was exciting and my parents loved me. I was really their only child. My sister, my only sibling, died at birth at the hospital and I never saw her.

I walked steadily, eager to see my mother. I had my book bag strapped to my back and carried my drawing in one hand so there was no chance of smudging the surface. I held it facing out and tried to be casual but I wanted the world to see what Miss Patchett had been so proud to display to her students, and what I was going to give my mother.

As I neared the corner to my home street off Elm, I saw Ruth, a girl who was a grade above and lived near the river. Usually her brother walked her home, and except for a few taunts, they usually ignored me. Her father was a doctor.

Today Ruth sat alone with her back against an oak tree, her books at her side. She was looking down at something in her hand. She was big for a girl, with strong, muscular legs and thick upper arms. She had short, dark brown hair and a wide, thick-lipped mouth with spaces between the teeth in front—not ugly really, but they held your attention. I circled around so as not to be close.

"That's a stupid bird," she called to me without looking at me.

I began to cross to the other side of the street, away from her. She stood up. She was in my art class. She must have remembered what Miss Patchett said about my bird.

"A really stupid, stupid bird." She stood, leaving her books, and came toward me. I moved quickly but she was too fast and she snatched my drawing and backed off. She had torn the bird into small pieces by the time I reached her.

My rage empowered me. With my fists I pummeled her, I pushed her down. I did not kick her, but I hit her again and again with my book bag, the brass buckles cutting her face and neck. Blood oozed from her forehead; she cried out and I hit her in the mouth with my fist, felt the pain as her teeth broke skin on my knuckles.

Two adults came. They held me from her. I tried to explain about the bird, but they saw me as unreasonable and out of control. I quieted and waited until Ruth's parents were found to take her to the hospital, and my mother came to get me.

Through tears I told mother about my bird, and she held me. I told her about my rage at Ruth destroying my gift without reason. And Mother said she loved me. But Ruth's parents demanded I be punished. The school was contacted to impose penalties—Ruth's parents thought I should be sent to reform school in New York. I was placed on probation and required to attend counseling sessions with my mother with the local pediatrician who had majored in psychology in college. The pediatrician was intent on reconciliation, and in time included Ruth's mother in some of the sessions with him and my mother. My mother and Ruth's mother came to an understanding and, I believe, liked each other in addition to gaining a mutual, if not at first hesitant, respect.

I survived my probation and my counseling. My family began to share family gatherings with Ruth and her parents, and her brother—who was much older than I.

It was a Saturday, and Ruth's parents had invited our family over for an afternoon barbecue. Ole Miss was playing LSU away and a radio had been propped on a windowsill of the house with the volume on maximum. The adults sat in folding lawn chairs around a brick lined barbecue pit with a pig on a spit that Ruth's father, the doctor, basted sauce on every few minutes. Ruth's brother went to shoot squirrels with a twenty-two near the dump, refusing to take Ruth and me. Ruth decided to fish on the river, a skill her brother had taught her, usually on the oxbow about a mile north. Ruth's mother insisted I tag along. Carrying her rod and tackle box, Ruth went to where the river narrowed, the surface white with froth swirling in eddies. I followed. There was a floating dock with a planked walkway that tilted up slightly now that the river was high from recent rains. The river grumbled and swished here. She stood at the dock's edge in her bare feet and cast a lure awkwardly upstream.

"Are there fish here?" I asked.

"There are millions of fish," Ruth said.

"Like brim?" I asked.

"All kinds. Like every kind in the whole world."

After that, she did not speak to me. I soon walked away back to the house. I threw a tennis ball for Ruth's father's black lab to retrieve. When it was time to eat, I was sent to tell Ruth. But there was no one on the dock. I returned to tell the adults.

"Where is she?" Ruth's mother said.

I didn't answer.

"Have you done something to her?"

"I'm sure she'll be here soon," my mother said, coming and standing close to me.

"You're an evil child," Ruth's mother said to me.

"That's not fair, Martha," my mother said. "He's done nothing."

But Ruth's mother, breathing fast through clenched teeth, was already sending people out in different directions to find Ruth.

"I'm sure everything is all right," my mother said, taking me with her as she followed Ruth's parents to the river. My father tended the grill.

An hour later, Ruth's body was lifted from the water a few hundred yards downstream. I stood back at the edge of the crowd, but I could see her face was scratched and her leg bruised. Her fishing rod was never found.

The sheriff questioned me on the day Ruth died. Then later, twice, once for three hours, I sat at the police station as we went over every second of that afternoon. But nothing happened and I went back to school in the fall. I thought life was as it should be, except that Ruth's parents never spoke to me and walked away when they saw me, even at school.

But life was not as I expected. Little things happened, which now seem unimportant, but that were etched into me. Adults looked over me when they talked where children were allowed, and teachers rarely called on me in class. In gym I was passed over when the teams were chosen, and even at Church in the children's choir when I usually sang my lead in "Down by the Riverside" from the front row next to the sopranos, I was told to stay in the back next to tone-deaf Arthur whom no one liked. Later that year "Just a Closer Walk with Thee" replaced "Down by the Riverside" and I had no solos.

My mother became my only confidant. I told her how I was treated. I told her I didn't care what people thought, but I did care and couldn't sleep well. I was haunted by formless nightmares with sensations of falling, prolonged and slow to wake me. On weekends, I often went alone to sit motionless and silently by the river —near where Ruth died. Mother had conferences with my teachers and the principal who seemed sympathetic and said I was a good boy and a hard worker.

They trusted me, they said. They definitely thought Ruth's mother's tirades against me about her daughter's death would stop, and soon be forgotten.

I graduated from high school in the top half of my class, but at the ceremony, when the principal handed me my diploma and shook my hand, his eyes never tried to see me as he did with others, looking instead beyond me to someone in the audience. My mother died when I was away in my third year in a Birmingham college and my father retired and moved to Florida with a woman he'd known since high school.

I did well enough in college to win a scholarship to pharmacy school. I've been in practice now for four years and I am manager of a drug store in Dayton, Ohio. I never speak of my past and I can't remember when, or if, anyone asked.

But I must tell my story now. I have a decision to make. A woman (Robyn Welter) loves me. She is a small, frail woman of thirty-five, two years older than I, quiet, gentle, and shy. She is a school librarian, and teaches English to fourth graders. I love her too, and we want to marry. A date has been set. But as the time has come closer, I cannot find it in me to want children. Robyn wants a family. It is what will fulfill her life. It has become a source of contention and many tears, and I have come to wonder if marriage is right for me. I do not want children. I do not want to see them grow up.

We have come to the church office of her minister here in Ohio, for consultation. She is religious, and I believe in God but have little faith in the church. Robyn and I sit in chairs in front of the minister's desk. He is a young, unmarried man with glasses and a nervous glance that lands on others at odd times, disjointed in some way, avoiding contact as if he couldn't face the realties he might see by looking into another's eyes. Robyn and the minister discuss our incompatibilities and after an awkward silence, I just tell my story without emotion. It is a slice of potential reality that I do not want to force on a child I foster. When I finish, Robyn expresses her love for me again, and looks immediately toward the minister who smiles and nods.

The minister mumbles something about perceptions and justice. Then his voice strengthens.

"I must be honest," he says, not looking at me, "You need to address this guilt. It seems to have consumed you. For a successful marriage, you must confront your inner demons."

I stare at him, not sure exactly of his meaning. I say nothing. I am not demonic.

He continues. "Your guilt frankly seems excessive for what you describe. Is there something that day by the river you might have repressed? Some nudge? Some hesitation to save her?"

I look to Robyn. It is, for her, the moment when she can make our marriage whole by believing in me. A marriage with children too. In her soul, she must know that even as a child I was incapable of murder, or even assisting in an accident. And that is what she must communicate to me.

She stares at me. At this instant I look into her eyes, tenuous in their lock on me, then she looks to her left, toward a table with a framed photo of a modern painting of Jesus in a romantic pose, holding a shepherd's crook. I continue to stare at Robyn, despair sweeping over me. She looks back. Now her eyes do not hold the sparkle and desire of our lovemaking. They hold pity. I slowly rise, button the front of my white lab coat, bow slightly to both if them.

"Don't run," the minister says.

"Please," Robyn says.

"Hypnosis," he says. "To explore your unconscious."

"You were a child," Robyn adds.

Who did nothing wrong, I want to tell her. But the well of doubt, once discovered, can never be erased.

"We could discover the facts," the minister says.

But we know the facts.

I exit to the street. I am surprised at how calm I am, still unaware of the weight of my resolution. I refuse to believe there is an evil memory inside me that will satisfy the omnipresent suspicions. I will bury myself in the demands of my profession. Alone, I will make my contributions to the world.

I pace away from the church until I am sweating, even though dark clouds swirl above and the chill of winter is already on us. I sit down on the low wall near the Air Force base. The street traffic is heavy. A near freezing rain begins to fall and the windshield wipers on cars that stop for the streetlight slap from side to side. I tremble, then sag, my arms are limp. "Bitch," I say. The minister is a fool. It is only Robyn, whom I love, who could pierce me with my own doubt about what I remember and what happened that day.

"I am without sin," I say aloud to a passing stranger who looks at me oddly without breaking stride.

Made in the USA
Lexington, KY
06 August 2010